INVASION OF THE RAT-MEN

I stepped into a doorway. The last stragglers of the panicked mob had pushed on by. I looked down the side street they had come from and saw something that made my heart sink: a crowd of the overcoated intruders, coming on at a run, running awkwardly, but amazingly swiftly, leaning forward at a perilous angle, their stubby legs twinkling below their long coat-skirts. One stumbled and fell and the rest flowed over him, leaving a shapeless heap behind. Then one turned back and ran to his fallen comrade and bent over him.

It took me a moment to realize he was eating him. . . .

Zone Yellow

An Imperium Novel

KEITH LAUMER

BAEN BOOKS

ZONE YELLOW

Copyright © 1990 by Keith Laumer

A Baen Books Original

Baen Publishing Enterprises
P.O. Box 1403
Riverdale, NY 10471

ISBN: 0-671-72028-7

Cover art by Tom Kidd

First printing, December 1990

Distributed by
SIMON & SCHUSTER
1230 Avenue of the Americas
New York, N.Y. 10020

Printed in the United States of America

Prologue

I decided to walk home from the big affair at the Richtofen palace; it was a mild evening for Stockholm in September, and I needed the exercise. When I turned off Strandvägen to take a shortcut via Styrmansgatan, I heard something behind me. I looked back, not feeling alarm, just mild curiosity. I caught only a glimpse of a tall, oddly narrow-shouldered figure wrapped to the ankles in a drab overcoat, just as he ducked into a side alley. That made me more curious. I went back as if casually, and as I reached the doorway, he literally fell on me. I threw him back and got a glimpse of an ugly, buck-toothed, chinless face just as he fell over sideways, and lay on the cobbles, moving feebly. I realized he really *had* fallen on me. He was wounded, or sick. I went to one knee to feel for a pulse. What I felt was a wiry wrist with a pelt like a terrier. I rolled him on his back; he had a rank rats-in-the-barn smell to him, plus a stink like rotten oranges. His clothes under the coat consisted of a closely-fitted coverall made of a woolly material. His long, deformed feet were in high-top shoes or low boots of a soft, wrinkled reddish leather. There was short fur on his shins.

His pockets were empty. The hair on the back of my neck was prickling, Nature's way of making me look bigger, to scare off predators. The rat-man's beady eyes were open and he was looking at me with an expression which, had he been human, I'd have called appealing. He mumbled something, all vowels and squeaks, ending with a moan. The light went out of the eyes. He was dead. A big, bristly Norway rat came scuttling along the alley, halted, sniffed, started around the dead creature, changed his mind and ran for it. I left the narrow alley and went back out to Strandvägen, where a mercury-vapor lamp shed a ghoulish light on the elegant facades facing the harbor and glittered on the choppy water. I saw a taxi with its cheery orange light on, and started toward it. The time of a leisurely stroll was past. I needed to get to *HQ, Kungliga Spionage*, ASAP.

When I was ten feet from the taxi, the cabby glanced at me, then gunned away from the curb and left me standing in a cloud of burnt-kerosene fumes. Stockholm's cabbies are known for their courtesy and helpfulness; something was bothering that fellow. I watched him speed across Gustav-Adolphstorg and into Tunnelgatan.

Just then, two men ran out of another side street. Well-dressed middle-aged Swedes don't jog around the city streets after dark. But these two were coming at full tilt, and there was another man running behind them, not chasing them, but fleeing from whatever had spooked the first two. Then a whole crowd burst from the narrow street, and I could hear the mob-roar coming from them. Some of them were bleeding from small wounds. They looked like a routed army. They kept coming, right past me, men and women and kids, all running hard, with terrified expressions on their faces. I went out to try to intercept one fellow, but he gave me a wild-eyed look and veered out around me. Over by the stone facade of an eighteenth-century ship's chandler something caught my eye, standing in a doorway: a tall, narrow figure like a six-foot, dull-olive cigar with feet and a turned-up collar. I felt panic grab at my throat and choked off the yell that I had spontaneously started to utter. Before I could so much as grab somebody and point out the stranger, I saw another one—then another. All three were simply standing in shadowy doorways. They were too tall, too narrow, with only feet showing beneath the long coats, and short, insignificant-looking arms with the hands tucked into high-set pockets. They were exactly like the ratty fellow who'd died in the alley. I didn't know why, but there was something indescribably ominous about these silent, unmoving fellows.

I stepped into a doorway. The last stragglers of the panicked mob had pushed on by. I looked down the side street they had come from and saw something that made my heart sink: a crowd of the overcoated intruders, coming on at a run, running awkwardly, but amazingly swiftly, leaning forward at a perilous angle, their stubby legs twinkling below their long coat-skirts. One stumbled and fell and the rest flowed over him, leaving a shapeless heap behind. Then one turned back and ran to his fallen comrade and bent over him.

It took me a moment to realize he was eating him.

The last few stragglers—I had stopped thinking of them as men—were having trouble keeping up, and tended to extend their arms and drop to all fours. If they were trying to overtake the mob, they didn't succeed, but they kept on coming, dozens, scores of them. They streamed past me without noticing me.

Then one fellow dropped out and scuttled over to a fire escape, which he went up, to the first landing, without slowing down. He stopped there and fumbled inside the drab coat and brought out something that I knew at once was a weapon, though it looked more like a wad of wire coathangers. He set himself and aimed it down across the *torg*, just above the last group of people, and a blue bolt of lightning slammed into the weathered stonework of the building above and ahead of them, and chunks of rock fell in their path, not quite blocking it. The mob skirted the obstruction, leaving behind three casualties writhing on the cobbles.

I eased out my old Walther 6.35, took aim, and put a round into the midsection of the shooter. He doubled over the rail and fell, twisting in midair. He hit hard, but his fellow whatever-they-weres went over or around him and left him there. Suddenly the plaza was empty, except for the casualties.

One of the three people injured by the falling stones had gotten to his feet and was exploring himself to find out how badly he was hurt. I went over to him. He gave me a startled look, but held his ground. He was a sturdy-looking young fellow in what looked to me like shore-clothes. He said,

"What the heck!" (Yes, "heck"; Swedes don't swear much.)

"How badly are you hurt?" I asked him.

He shook his head vaguely. "What happened?" he continued. "I was running—"

"Why?"

"The rat-men," he said. "Didn't you see them? Everybody was running and I didn't have any better idea, so I joined in." He touched his left arm. "Just a broken arm, it appears," he diagnosed. He looked at the middle-aged woman and the elderly man lying on the pavement beside us, bloody. Both were dead.

"*They* weren't so lucky," he commented. He glanced at the reddish stone fragments, then looked up at the wound on the store-front. "Artillery fire. Who—?" He broke off and gave me a hard look. "*You're* not running," he accused. "Friends of yours?"

I knew he meant the rat-men; I denied it, and pointed to the one I'd shot. "He was the one who dropped the rocks on you," I told him. He nodded and went over toward the dead creature. The light of the street lamps was wan in the colorless stone plaza, surrounded by drab age-worn facades. His feet echoed. Otherwise the silence was complete, except for some yells in the distance. My eye fell on a handbill stuck on the lamppost: *Sätt in på blodbanken. Du kan själv behöver ta ut* (Deposit in the bloodbank. You might need to make a withdrawal). That harmless exhortation suddenly had a personal and ominous meaning for me. I went on to where the man with the broken arm was looking down at the dead thing, wrapped in its dowdy coat. He rolled it on its back, or tried to; its long, slinky build wouldn't let it stay put. It flopped back to its half-curled position on one side.

"This thing is not human," he remarked, sounding shocked. He flipped the coat open, exposing a sort of body-stocking of the same mousey color as the wool coat. The arms, which we could see clearly now, were abnormally short and stubby, and the hands were like bones covered with pinkish leather, talon-tipped.

"You called them 'rat-men,'" I reminded him.

He sniffed and nodded. "I've smelled enough ship-rats to recognize the stink," he grunted. "Look here," he went on urgently. "This has to be reported to the authorities."

"Sure," I agreed. "I was on my way to Imperial Intelligence."

"Why them?" he wanted to know. "Why not the police?"

"It's only a block or two," I countered. "And the cops wouldn't know any more about this than we do. I think it's an item for Net Surveillance."

"You mean that spook outfit that explores 'alternate realities' or something?"

"Certainly," I confirmed the obvious. "And in this case a very distant one, where the primates lost out to the rodents back in the Cretaceous."

"I'm just a simple nuclear engineer," my new friend objected. "I don't know anything about all that 'Net' business—and the little I *do* know, I doubt! 'Alternate worlds,' hah! One is enough! It doesn't make sense, from an engineering viewpoint!"

"Then the viewpoint needs work."

"It doesn't work," he stated, like a fellow getting set for a pub debate. "If there are alternate realities, we'd be surrounded by them, and if they differed from one A-line to its neighbor if only in some detail, like, in one the ship sank, and in another it reached Iceland—" (I realized he'd read more about the Net than he was letting on) "—they'd have the same technology you say *we* have, and our analogs would be swarming all over the place, running into each other—or even themselves!"

I shook my head, "No, because the Net technology involves meddling with the basic energies that generate what we think of as reality—"

"Think of, hell!" he cut in. "Reality *is* reality; not a matter of opinion!"

"Is yesterday 'reality'?" I asked him. He started to give a quick answer, but paused instead, and I said, " 'Tomorrow'?"

He frowned at me. "*Ja visst!*" he said uncertainly. "It's just that yesterday is past and tomorrow hasn't happened yet."

"What about now?" I hit him with next.

"No doubt about it!" he stated flatly, still frowning as he looked down at the dead thing at our feet. "I *think*," he amended.

"The present moment," I pointed out, "is merely the intersection of the past and the future; it has no temporal dimension. *Everything* is in either the past or the future, like a sheet of paper cut in two: every molecule of paper is in one half or the other."

"What's that got to do—?" he began.

I waved that away. "Maxoni and Cocini were lucky, in our continuum. Amazingly lucky. They didn't blow our line out of existence. In all the nearby lines, they did, or they failed completely, so we're not bumping into our alternate selves bent on the same errand. Though I did meet my alter ego once in a place we call Blight-Insular Two.

"It's a region where the experiments went awry," I told him, "it dissolved the temporal fabric so as to destroy causality, disrupt the regular entropic flow, and so on. Disasters of every kind befell the affected lines. But there are a couple of surviving islands in the Blight. More or less normal lines very close to and similar to this, the Zero-zero line."

He nodded, not as if he was convinced. "How do you happen to know about all this?" he thought to ask.

"I'm Colonel Bayard of Imperial Intelligence. I've been in some of those A-lines. Crossed the Blight more than once. I assure you it's true. *This* Stockholm—" I glanced across the plaza at the solid, real, clearly-the-only-one-of-its-kind city. "Stockholm Zero-zero—is only one of a literally infinite manifold of parallel universes, each differing from the adjacent lines in perhaps no more than the relative positions of two grains of sand on the beach—or even of two molecules within one grain of sand. Don't worry, your analogs in the closely adjacent lines are just as sure as you are that what my analogs are telling them is nonsense."

"You mean . . ." he stammered, the dead thing at his feet forgotten, "that I—that there are—?" He couldn't quite say it. It was understandable: he was just a normal citizen, who'd heard vaguely of Net Operations, without ever really boning up on the subject, any more than the average citizen pokes into the details of space technology.

"Exactly," I told him. "As choices between alternatives come up, both occur; the lines split, and each probability-line carries on independently. When you last had to make a decision at a crossroads, you went *both* ways—and on to separate destinies. So did everybody else. The amount of difference that develops depends on the time since the Common History date. I spent some time in one of the lines where Napoleon won at Waterloo. C.H. date 1815."

"But . . . how—?" He couldn't seem to complete a sentence, but I understood; I had felt the same way, all those years ago when poor Captain Winter had grabbed me off the street a few blocks from here and told me the same crazy story.

Since then I'd learned to accept it, even become a part of the organization that maintained surveillance over the vast continuum of worlds opened up by the M-C drive, which enabled us to move at will *across* the lines. The drive is the basis for the Imperium itself, the government centered here at the Zero-zero coordinates of the Net, maintaining peace and order among the lines.

I resumed my explanation. "There were many Net-traveling lines, of course, those very close to the Zero-zero, where Maxoni and Cocini had perfected their strange device without incurring the disaster that had created the Blight—"

"I've heard of 'the Blight.' " My new pal broke in on my explanation. "Some kind of desert, isn't it, where everything's gone wrong?"

"That's putting it mildly. The energies involved in the drive are the same ones that power the eternal creation/destruction cycle of reality. If they're not tightly channeled, chaos results: cinder worlds where all life was destroyed when the suns exploded; hell-worlds of radiation and earthquakes, and even worse, lines where life went awry, and great masses of protoplasm, some human, grow like immense tumors, spreading across the land, or where horribly mutated plants and animals engage in a never-ending struggle to eat each other—all the way down to pleasant places you'd mistake for home, except that the United Colonies were absorbed by Spain in 1898. Or perhaps where the Kaiser formed an alliance with his cousins Czar Alexander and King Edward the Seventh, destroyed the French Republic, and restored the Bourbon dynasty in 1914. Or even a line where you missed a streetcar and never met your wife and went on to become a world-famous movie star, or—"

"I understand," he cut me off. "I mean, I don't under*stand*, but—" His eyes went to the sprawled animal in the overcoat. "How could a thing like this exist?"

"Way back," I guessed, "the Cretaceous, the beginning of the Age of Mammals, our small, shrew-like progenitor apparently lost the competition for the tree-habitat to the smaller rat-like critters, and a hundred million years later, this"—I prodded the corpse with my foot—"is the result."

"But how did it get *here*? By the way"—he interrupted himself to thrust out a hand to me, as if he felt a sudden need to reestablish contact with the human race—"I'm Lars Burman. I was just on my way home, and . . ." He let that one die, too. I shook his hand.

"His species clearly has a drive like the M-C," I said. "Why he's here, so far from his native climes, is a tough one. He's not alone, you know. I saw a mob of at least a hundred or so; this fellow fell out to do some killing and got himself killed."

"How did he—?" Lars interrupted himself as usual. "You said he brought the stones down on me."

I picked up the weapon he'd used, a hybrid of a bent coathanger and a compound crossbow, with exposed wiring, and no clear indication of which was the business end. I showed it to Burman.

"With this," I told him. He nodded as if I'd said something sensible and took the thing. Clearly, *he* knew which was the business end; the engineer in him, no doubt.

"Interesting," he commented. "The principle —I'm not sure, of course—but I'd guess this is based on control of the weak nuclear force—no wonder it knocks chunks out of solid granite. Very sophisticated. We've been working along these lines for some time." He handed it back; I took it carefully. He showed me how to hold it and pointed out the trigger.

By this time a few people had appeared, opening doors and venturing cautiously out. They saw us and came our way, calling questions before they got in conversational range. We didn't have any answers. A young woman went to the two dead people and started sobbing. Then we all heard a yell from the middle distance and looked that way. A man with blood on his face was staggering toward our little group of strangers. Burman and a couple of others went to meet him and guide him over. I don't know why; we couldn't help him. The bloody nose advanced uncertainly. His eyes were on the dead thing.

"More of them on the way—lots more!" he gasped. "They're coming out of the old coal cellars at the shipyards. I fell," he added apologetically, wiping his nose and spreading the crimson stain around. "I saw them kill a man—shoot him—with one of *those!*" He pointed to the gadget I was holding. "Blew him apart!" he blurted, and gagged. "It was horrible! He never had a chance! Just a rag-picker, poking around in the rubbish-bin. They killed him like a rat!"

The crowd decided we knew no more than they did, and began moving off, in twos and threes; nobody went alone. A lone rat-man came out of one of those narrow side streets by the old shipyard; he seemed to be in trouble; he was staggering in a comical way on his stubby legs; he stopped to look around, and started our way.

"It's not armed, I think," Lars said. I agreed.

"I've got a pistol," I told him. "You'd better take this thing." I handed him the alien weapon. Ten feet away, the critter stopped to look us over. The beady eyes in the pointed, ratty face flicked over us, stopped at the weapon Burman was holding. It was definitely sniffing. It held out a narrow, long-fingered hand, and made a squeaky sound, like a rusty hinge.

Burman said, "Keep back," in a mild tone, then, to me, "It makes the hair on my neck stand up."

The thing squeaked again, more urgently, if I could read human tones in a rusty hinge.

"Who are you?" I asked, just to be saying something.

"You are nod of our trusted cadre," the thing said in a high-pitched, but comprehensible voice. "Why do you have tisrupdor?" Its eyes flicked to the dead one. "You dreacherously killed Tzl and doog his sidearm," it accused.

"I sure as hell did, weasel-puss," I replied, and eased my Walther into quick-draw position. "Your pal Seal killed two people, and would have killed more."

" 'Tzl,' " the thing corrected. "Gan none of you mongs learn to speag gorregly?"

"Why should we?" I demanded. "This is *our*

world—" I got that far before he flipped his disruptor into working position. It fit his stubby-armed physique perfectly, which is why it was awkward for Lars, who nonetheless had aimed his disruptor at the alien before it had its weapon at the ready.

"Repend, slaves!" the alien said, in its squeaky but grammatically perfect upper-class English.

"We're not slaves, rat-head," Lars told it, quite calmly. "Now: who are you, *what* are you, and why are you here?"

"I have high honor to be Pack Commander Qzk," it said, enunciating carefully. "I am not obliged to endure interrogation by scum, but I will tell you, since you appear so appallingly ignorant, that I represent the Central Command of Ylokk, and I am here, with my troopers, to clear native creatures from this urban area. Now, you!" it addressed Burman, ignoring me and my automatic. "Give me that weapon!"

"If you say so, sir," Lars said humbly, and blew a hole in Commander Qzk big enough to hide a football (soccer-type) in, knocking the arrogant alien for a six-foot slide on his back, after he hit the cobbles. Lars looked at me as if expecting a rebuke.

"As well now as later," I told him. "Now we *have* to get to HQ, fast, with this information." I started off, passing the two dead 'Locks,' I think he had called his kind, and the two dead people. So far, the score was even.

Going along the deserted streets, we saw more of the rat-men, mostly in pairs, once a patrol of ten, once a lone critter leaning against a wall and puking. None of them saw us ducking along from shadow to shadow. We reached HQ; the wrought-iron pole-lamps flanking the granite steps were on, and lights burned behind a few windows, but no one, human or alien, was in sight.

There was no guard in the sentry-box inside, either. It was very still, but I thought I heard voices far away, from somewhere above. We went up the marble staircase and along the wide corridor to Richtofen's office. Again, no sentry on duty. I rapped and an irritable voice snapped.

"You may enter!"

I did, with Lars at my heels, and a burly security type I'd met before aimed a machine pistol at my dinner and said, "Oh, it's you, colonel. Good. The general wants to see you."

"Aim that thing at your foot, Helge," I replied. "This is Lars Burman. He's on our side—and it's a good thing, because if he weren't, he'd have blown you in two with that coathanger he's holding."

Helge lowered his weapon rather sheepishly, put out a hand for the disruptor, pulled it in again and nodded at the inner door. Before we reached it, it opened, and Manfred von Richtofen was standing there, gray-haired, immaculate in his Net Surveillance Service uniform, getting just a little stooped now—he was past eighty. He held out a hand and said, "I thought it was you, Brion. Good. Welcome. Come in, and Mr. Burman as well."

I shook his hand and so did Lars.

"What the hell's going on, sir?" I asked him. "Where are they coming from?" Richtofen waved a hand at a wall map of the city, which was built on an archipelago, the islands linked by bridges. There were red and yellow pins stuck in it in a pattern of concentric arcs centered on the waterfront, near where I'd met my first rat-man.

"It's a trans-Net invasion, Brion," he said grimly. "No doubt about that."

"How many are there?" was my next question.

"No firm estimate," he told me. "Not enough data. But a steady stream of reinforcements is arriving. Casualties are light, so far, because we haven't mounted any organized resistance. They seem to be trying to capture a few people at random, when they happen to encounter them. The first report came in from Göteborg, about an hour ago. A hot-line call, just about the time you were leaving the party. I sent a detail after you, to inform you, but they missed you."

"I took a shortcut," I explained.

"Still, you're here now," Richtofen said, as if that solved everything.

"Why don't we call out the local garrison and round them up?" I wanted to know.

"It's a full-scale invasion," the general said grumpily. "We can't hit them all at once. In the city alone, there are hundreds of confirmed sightings so far." He waved at the map with pins.

"Red for casualties, yellow for just sightings," he explained. "Whoever they are, they mean business. My technical chief, Sjöman—you've met him of course, Brion—tells me they're from a line far outside our surveillance zone."

"Have you seen one up close, sir?" I asked him.

He shook his head. "No prisoners yet. They have potent hand weapons and they're not averse to using them. They've repulsed every man who tried to parley with them. I saw two from across the street out front," he added. "Sneaky-looking fellows; strange hunched-forward way of walking. And one was on all fours for a moment, I'm almost sure."

"He was," I confirmed. "Those things aren't human, Manfred." I handed him the disruptor.

"This is what they're doing their shooting with. No, the other way. Careful! It can blow the side out of the building. Better get Sjöman in here. Lars can explain the thing to him."

Richtofen handled the weapon with respect and pushed a button on his desk that brought the tech chief in at a run. Richtofen handed over the disruptor and Lars went over to him and said, "Fortunately, sir, it's a type of weapon that will be easy to negate. It projects a field of energy, and with a slight adjustment, it can be made to project an out-of-phase field that cancels the basic field when it impinges on it. We need to run off a batch of them as soon as possible."

Sjöman was nodding as if that meant something.

"How much territory have they secured, General?" I wanted to know.

"You're very formal tonight, Brion," Richtofen replied in mild rebuke. "Here in Stockholm, they've taken over the Old Town for some reason, and Södra, and are rapidly clearing the center of the city. They've set up a field HQ on Kungsgatan near Stureplan. We've killed a few hundred of them. They seem heedless of our gunfire—walk right into it."

An aide rushed in just then with a report that confirmed the aliens were swarming in every city and town so far contacted, as well as in Paris, Copenhagen, Oslo, and every other capital on the continent. London reported fighting in the streets. No word yet from North America. No contact with Japan.

"Communications have virtually collapsed," Richtofen told us. "These fellows know just what to go after. Bridges and airfields sealed off, transmitter towers down, highways blocked. What news we've had has come by sea. It's as if they were unaware of travel by sea. Our ships come and go freely. They seem to be limiting their attention pretty much to the urban areas, but they're in the small towns, too. Very few have been seen in rural areas, except in scattered groups. They're apparently more interested in driving the people out of towns than in killing them; casualties have occurred mostly when people get in their way. Those who flee are allowed to go, then rounded up and detained."

"That makes it a little difficult," I commented. "We can't use heavy weapons on them without destroying our own cities."

"Precisely," Richtofen agreed. "I assume that's the basis for their strategy."

"How many of them would you say we're dealing with?" I asked.

"My best guess is about four hundred thousand, at this point," Richtofen said grimly. "And more arriving every hour."

"Make that three hundred ninety-nine thousand, nine hundred ninety-eight," Lars contributed.

"It appears," Manfred said seriously, "that our best strategy is to resort to guerrilla warfare. I've already taken steps to establish a field HQ near Uppsala. You and Barbro had better get up there right away. I'm counting on you to take command."

I said, "Yessir," but with a sinking feeling.

1

During the course of the next twenty-four hours, we got a few Imperial Army units mobilized, equipped with hastily run off wide-field anti-disruptor beams. We made up a six-truck convoy, and forced our way through some flimsy Ylokk barricades to the open countryside with no casualties —on our side. By "we," I mean Barbro, Luc, our loyal houseman, a dozen or so senior officers of the Army and the NS service, their families, various doctors, mechanics, cooks, a pick-up squad of men on leave, and anybody else who wanted to evacuate, most of them carrying along a few unleave-behindables.

At the edge of the city we commandeered six buses and an Army half-track, and after repulsing repeated feeble attacks, soon gathered in enough men to fill our transport.

"These 'Lock' aren't what you'd call crack troops,"

a young lieutenant named Helm commented. He'd served in the peace-keeping force in the Middle East, and he'd seen determined attacks. These fellows seemed tired, half-hearted by comparison. That was OK with me. But they were persistent, and didn't seem to mind casualties, though they always dragged their dead and wounded away when they fell back, and always they managed to snag a few prisoners.

Once we were clear of the city's outskirts, the aliens stopped harassing us. Our new gadgets had worked fine, and since the enemy seemed to have specialized in the one, seemingly irresistible weapon, they soon learned to run when we appeared. It was a stand-off: they got the cities; we could have the country. It was peaceful there, but somehow it didn't look the same. We saw a few evidences of war.

2

We were directed to Field HQ in a clearing in a beech forest near a small town. On the way, we encountered a roadblock adorned with three wrecked trucks, and a 75mm Bofors. The gun crews were ready to blow our lead bus off the road until I and a couple of other plainly human fellows jumped down and convinced the troops we were the good guys. They sounded glad to see us after they got over their disappointment at not getting to use their field-gun on the buses, but they kept staring down the road the way we'd come. They told us about a shortcut to Headquarters. We found it: a six-man tent and a half-track with a few Army men standing around.

I took over from an exhausted brigadier who was almost out on his feet, but was doing his best to monitor the action around and in the city, and to keep the few local levies he'd managed to get together in position to block any further advance into the area.

An anxious-looking major came in from the woods and asked me, "Where's the main body, sir?" He didn't quite break into tears when I said, "We're it."

"We've turned back one small convoy so far," he told me. "They drove right into our gun muzzle. Didn't seem to realize what it was. They've got some heavy stuff of their own, but very short-range." He pointed out a couple of smashed tree-stumps a hundred feet from the tent. "They blew them up, but didn't come any farther, after we blew two lorry-loads off the road." He patted the flank of the half-track with its Bofors .80.

"They're used to short-range energy weapons," I explained to him. "That gives us a sort of advantage, if we can entice them out of town. Carry on, major; I'll be back."

The major nodded, and said, "*Ja visst!* We can't use our gun in the city; we'd destroy it!"

I told him to keep up the good work, and I took some men and went out to reconnoiter, cautiously. I didn't think the Ylokk would be taking their rebuff at the roadblock lightly. We could see their patrols, single scouts and details of up to ten men—oops!—things, clustered around every outbuilding and thicket. We moved on, three of our vehicles limping badly, and soon came in sight of the little town called Sigtuna. It looked peaceful as Swedish towns always look on a spring morning. There was a burnt-out half-track in the ditch half a mile from the first building, a dun-colored restaurant with red geraniums in window boxes. I checked inside: nobody alive there. A hundred yards farther on, we found a man in Swedish Army gray-green, lying in the middle of the road. He stirred as my lead truck came up and stopped beside him. He had a terrible wound in the leg. I got down and went to him in time to hear him say:

"Look out, colonel. They—" He went limp then and I couldn't find a pulse. Just before I left him I noticed his left hand had been gnawed, as if by rats. Not a nice way to go, eaten alive by the rat-men of Ylokk.

3

When we moved on into downtown, there were a couple of ineffectual attacks on us by foot-troops. They didn't have much of what the French call *élan*: they charged from concealment behind the hedgerows in a lackadaisical way, then fell back as soon as we fired into them. Their short-range weapons didn't touch us.

Sigtuna was quiet; there were a few people in sight, and no Ylokk. They'd been there, though—there was enough merchandise scattered in the streets, and smashed store windows, to make it clear there'd been looting. We saw a few dead aliens and one dead man, a fat fellow in a provincial constable's uniform.

A staff car flying the Monitor Service flag came out of a side street and waited for us. I leaned out and a fellow I'd seen around Net Surveillance

25

headquarters in Stockholm got out, came over and saluted. He needed a shave.

"Captain Aspman reporting, sir," he told me. "I've got a command post set up in a restaurant there." He pointed to one with phlox in the window boxes. "We were just getting ready to start worrying, Colonel," he added.

"You can go ahead and worry now, Captain," I told him. "Things seem to be under control here," I added.

"I hope so, sir," Aspman said. "We got here ahead of them and beat them back rather easily. The little news I've gotten from the rest of the country isn't so good, though. They're taking over— and operating—power plants, airports, fuel and supply warehouses. It seems they plan to live off the land. And, sir, they're cannibals! They take all the prisoners they can—probably to eat."

"Not really, Captain," I corrected him. "They're not human, so eating men isn't cannibalism for them."

"I know, sir, but they eat their own dead—and wounded." He sounded shocked. "I put one fellow out of his misery. He'd been shot in the belly, and his comrades had eaten off his left arm." Aspman shuddered. "I hate these things, Colonel! What are we going to do about them?" He sounded as if he really didn't know.

"Easy, Captain," I said. "We're going to get organized and eliminate them—or drive them back to where they came from."

Aspman nodded. "Certainly, sir—but—"

"How many men do you have here, Captain?" I asked him. He didn't know exactly. I told him to find out and to give me a complete inventory of supplies on hand, plus full information on the civilians trapped in the town, and, of course everything he'd managed to learn about the Ylokk force besieging Sigtuna. He gave me a semi-snappy salute and took off.

I found an empty room in the back of the hotel/restaurant and had my stuff brought in to set up my ops room. In a few minutes Aspman's couriers started arriving with bits and pieces of the information I needed, either verbally reported or scribbled on odd bits of paper. I called Aspman in.

"Collate all this information as it comes in, organize and consolidate it, and give me a clear typed copy," I told him. "Get on the ball, Captain," I added. "We don't have time for SNAFU right now."

He left, protesting about something. Just then Barbro came in; I'd left her helping some of the local women with kids, who needed shelter and food. She looked at the heap of scrap paper on my desk and started right in. In five minutes I had a nice clean list of military supplies on hand, and five minutes later one on the civilian or privately-owned food, matériel, clothing, and spare rooms. Aspman came back, his hands full of more scribbled paper.

"It can't be done, sir!" he was complaining. Barbro took a piece of paper from the wad in his hand, smoothed it out, glanced at it and said, "These blankets are just what Herr Borg keeps in the window," she told him crisply. "There's another gross in his warehouse, under the tarps."

"I didn't have time—" Aspman started. "Anyway, who—?" He broke off, looking resentfully at my gorgeous red-headed wife.

"That's all for you, mister," I said. "You can turn in your captain's insignia right now, and I'll try to find something useful for you to do here in the office." I glanced at the stuff in the teakwood containers by my desk. "Maybe emptying wastebaskets," I suggested.

"Look here!" Aspman blurted. "My commission comes directly from His Majesty the King! No mere foreigner can take it from me!"

Barbro went over to him and said, "Surely, sir, the success of the mission outweighs personal considerations. Please follow your orders."

He looked at his feet and muttered. I took his arm and lifted him high enough to look at his face.

"I can't afford to tolerate incompetents, mister," I told him. "I need an adjutant who can get things done and done right—in a hurry. Now get out of here!" I threw him halfway to the door; he scuttled the rest of the way. I glanced at Barbro. "It had to be done," I apologized. "This is war."

"But, Brion," she replied, "who do you have to replace him?"

"How about you?" I suggested. "I need these supplies collected and warehoused, fast."

She gave me a sardonic salute—she was a captain in the NSS Reserve—and left with no questions.

The next couple of hours were a nightmare. Aspman had done nothing constructive during his tenure. The military personnel (two hundred reservists) were in a state of confusion, not even knowing their units or officers. Most of them hadn't been issued a uniform or a weapon, or even been fed regularly. The townspeople were alienated and uncooperative, thanks to Aspman's high-handed methods and self-promotion. He'd kicked the local

banker out of his villa and made it his personal
property. I had a hard time even getting a few
citizens to talk to me. Most of them seemed to
have no idea of what was happening. Several hadn't
even seen one of the invaders. No wonder they'd
been uncooperative with Aspman's autocratic methods. So I made a speech.

4

"People, we're faced with the worst disaster ever to confront the Imperium: invasion, on a large scale, by non-human creatures who apparently intend to take over our world. They're in all the major cities we've heard from. But we're a long way from helpless. We have defense forces and trained and well-armed troops. They'll be here soon. In the meantime we have to do all we can to hold the enemy off. Sigtuna has been selected as the headquarters for our defense in this province. Other forces are deploying elsewhere. I was placed in command of the defense here, and I need good men and women to help me. First I have to requisition stores of supplies to support our effort. I have lists here which I'll distribute in a few minutes. Now, I'm calling for volunteers to man collection stations."

A plump, middle-aged fellow spoke up. "Collect what?" he demanded.

"Whatever is in the town that we need in order to fight the Ylokk," I told him.

"What's this 'lock'?" he wanted to know.

"We've determined that 'Ylokk' is the name by which the non-human invaders call themselves."

"Non-*what*?" somebody yelled.

"The Ylokk are not human beings," I explained. "They appear to be rodentia, descendants of highly-evolved rat-like ancestors dating back to the Cretaceous era."

"I saw one fellow, looked human to me," a thin woman shrilled. "This is just an excuse to justifying killing harmless strangers!"

"How close did you see him?" I interrupted her.

"Half a block," she grumped. "Human as I am. Wearing an overcoat and everything!"

"If you'd seen one as close as I have, you'd know they're not human," I assured her. "In any case, we are certainly not going to stand idly by while they take over our country."

A burly young fellow stood up. "I saw two of 'em break down the door to the grocery," he said. "Knocked a man down; heard screams from inside, and an explosion, sounded like. Human or not, we can't put up with that stuff right here in our own town! I'm volunteering, Colonel, for whatever I can do to help throw 'em out."

Others spoke up, pro and con. A few who had gotten a better look at the rat-men tried to tell the others about them, but were met with surprisingly vigorous resistance, based on the theory that the Government was persecuting poor immigrants. Finally, I put an end to the debate by using a chair on two hard-looking fellows who had eased up to me and tried to hustle me. The chair was a light steel folding one, but it sent both of them back to regroup. Then I had to draw my issue pistol and put a round through the ceiling to get everybody's attention. The room was in a near-riot condition, but they got quiet in a hurry when a shot was fired. A meaty fellow with a bloody nose pushed through to confront me.

"Go ahead, shoot me!" he challenged. "Your fascist tricks won't work here!"

"Go tend to that nose," I told him. "I don't intend to shoot anybody but the enemy. I never met a Fascist. Mussolini's been dead a long time."

He snorted and turned to face the roomful of excited citizens, and started to make a speech. I spun him around by the coat collar.

"I don't know who you are, Fats," I told him, "and I don't give a damn. Sit down and shut up." I gave him a hearty shove to help him on his way. He tripped and fell on his back, and looked up, squalling. A fellow with a bleeding scalp jumped forward to help him up. "Here, Mr. Borg, let me just give you a hand here," he gobbled, and gave me a dirty look. Borg got up with no difficulty, and ran along the wall to the door and out. The thin woman who had insisted the Ylokk were just harmless strangers darted after him. The noise level abated a little.

"Listen to me!" I had to yell to be heard. "This is war! *We're* going to win it. If anyone here is in doubt as to which side he's on, he'd better make up his mind right now. All in favor of lying down and letting these rats take over, move over to this side, please!"

Feet shuffled, but nobody moved.

"Fine," I said. "Now that that's settled, let's get to work."

I gave them a résumé of our resources: a hundred and fifty more-or-less trained troops, two hundred and ten townspeople, and another eighty-five refugees from Stockholm and other places, including too many women, kids, and elderly men. We had our six buses and five heavy trucks (one had broken an axle), and few local cars, and four light trucks; one field piece with fifty rounds, twenty-six hunting rifles, six revolvers, with a few rounds each, plus ten of the new anti-disruptor gadgets. Plenty of water from the town's system; a warehouse half full of food, mostly canned goods; assorted blankets; extra clothing and so on. The Swedish weather is inclined to be cold all of a sudden.

"We're in pretty good shape to hold our own," I told them. "We can't stand a long siege. The garden vegetables will have to be rationed, starting now."

"Say," a lean, hayseed type yelled. "Them's *my* vegetables yer talking about."

I told him he'd be compensated and he calmed down. Funny how people can keep their minds on money when their entire way of life, and life itself, are at hazard.

Lars Burman came in about then; I'd sent him out to reconnoiter to give us an idea of how many of the enemy were in the area.

"We're bottled up," he blurted before I could shush him. "They've encircled the town, occupied the close farmhouses, and set up roadblocks all around. There's hundreds of them, maybe thousands! We won't be getting any reinforcements, it appears." By now my little meeting was in near-riot condition again.

I soothed them, told them I'd have jobs for all of them, and questioned Lars more closely about troop dispositions. They had set up a thin line all the way around town; easy to punch through, if we'd had anywhere to go. They didn't seem to care about the field HQ in the tent.

"For the present," I told my audience, over their muttering, "we'll sit tight and leave the next move to them."

A fat old fellow who'd been an army officer bustled forward. "We can assume they'll close in after they think we've been sufficiently weakened by hunger and nervous stress," he told me. "They'll advance along the main streets into town, and that's where we have to be waiting for them. I suggest we place our eighty-eight-millimeter in the square, where it can be swiveled to command whatever street they come on."

I agreed with him, and picked ten able-bodied fellows in the crowd as squad leaders, telling them to recruit up to fifty volunteers each, arm them as well as possible, position them in the side streets, and be ready to flank any advancing column that appeared.

Lars came back from looking out the window. "Farmhouse or barn on fire to the east," he reported. "Lots of the rats swarming over that way, too."

A little man who'd been making a lot of noise uttered a wail. "That's *my* house!" he yelled at us as if I'd ordered it burned. He started for the door. I asked him where he was going.

He turned and gave me a hurt look. "I'm not

going to stand here while those *animals* destroy my place!" he yelled. There were a few faint cheers.

"What do you intend to do about it?" I wanted to know.

"I've got a weapon," he told me, and patted his coat pocket. "I'll take a few of the vermin with me . . . and maybe . . ." He trailed off. He hadn't quite realized he was committing suicide.

"Stick around," I suggested, "and you can help do something effective."

"Guess I'd better," he conceded. He went to the window and turned and yelled that now the barn was gone, and it was too late to save the house, so what was it I had in mind. He whirled back to the window, which was open. "Listen!" he yelled. I did so. There were sounds of farmcarts on brick pavement, and shouts. I went over. Ex-captain Aspman was down there in the courtyard apparently organizing some sort of convoy of wagons hitched to shaggy northern ponies, loaded with our most strategically important supplies. I wondered where he thought he was going.

I called down to him, "Hold everything right there, Aspman!"

"Like hell I will, damn you!" he shouted back. "I'm going to save the people of Sigtuna, even though *you* intend to betray them!"

That was all it took: the roomful of civic leaders behind me all tried at once to climb on top of me. I had to hold them off without hurting anybody. Then they formed up in a semicircle with its end against the wall on either side of me and just out of reach. The shrill little woman who, I'd realized, ran the local social scene was front and center.

"You all heard what the captain said," she yelled. "That's him,"—she pointed at me—"right there—

the stranger who came bursting into our city and is trying to take over, so he can sell us out to the strangers—strangers, like him!" With that off her flat chest, she subsided to muttering.

I took the opportunity to try to say something. "I'm Colonel Bayard of the Net Surveillance Service. I've been appointed by General Baron von Richtofen to assume command of this Field Headquarters, and this is it! Aspman is a fool and I had to relieve him, so just calm down and start doing what needs to be done."

"So you're the big man, eh?" the old witch cackled. "Let's see some papers to prove that, feller! Anyways, I never heard o' this Net Survey and all!"

"There wasn't time to issue written orders," I told them, feeling like someone offering lame excuses. "But while we stand here and gab, the Ylokk are making their troop dispositions. I say let's interfere a little! You—" I pointed to the fellow who'd jumped me earlier. "You like to get rough; come with me and I'll give you something to get rough with." He stepped forward and opened his mouth to tell me to go to hell, but just then we all heard a yell from down below. I was first to look down into the courtyard; it was swarming with aliens, who had already pushed the carts over and herded the dozen or so men back into one corner. Aspman was dithering; then he drew a pistol he'd gotten from somewhere and before he could fire it, a rat-man flattened him with a disruptor. The people behind me screamed. "Why, they *killed* Captain Aspman! Look! He's dead! His insides—"

The next moment they were all yelling at me to *do* something. I told them to calm down and wait for further instructions, and went down to the courtyard. The rat-men were still crowding in through the open gate that I had locked an hour before. I could see them in the street where the roadblocks had been removed, advancing unimpeded, the nearest only a few yards away. I pushed past an overturned cart and collared the uniformed sergeant who was taking over for Aspman and asked him what the hell was going on. I had to yell to be heard, and I used my dress saber on one Ylokk who seemed to have picked me as his special project.

"Had to get out, Cap'n said," the sergeant told me, at the same time putting a slug into the midsection of a tall, lean alien with three-inch incisors. "Said how the big shots were grabbing all the food and guns for themselves, and planned to make a deal with the enemy to let 'em have the townspeople in return for—"

"That's all lunatic ravings, Sergeant. Who unlocked the gate?"

"I did, sir; Cap'n's order, sir, to clear the way so we could make a run for it, sir."

"You also removed the barricades, I suppose," I said.

He nodded. "Had to move fast, Cap'n said." He glanced at Aspman's messy remains. "Guess Cap'n was wrong, sir. But he had the rank, and—"

"You did what you had to do, Sarge," I comforted him. "Didn't you think about the fact that you were opening a way in as well as out?"

"Cap'n said . . . they wouldn't advance, had a deal with you, sir. I see now he was lying, just wanted to save his own sweet butt."

"What about the guard detail at the city gate?" was my next query.

"Called 'em in," the non-com admitted. "They're here, somewhere, I guess." He looked around the crowded yard, where the Ylokk had now subdued all but two small groups of bleeding men, herding them into corners, and leaping it to bite, rather than using their weapons. The men were still firing, bringing down the Ylokks until their corpses formed makeshift breastworks. A few of the aliens had abandoned the attack and were now crouched, nibbling on their own dead. They ignored the human corpses. Apparently they liked rat meat better. I wondered why they were taking so many prisoners.

I gave the Sergeant his instructions and told him to get through to one of the embattled squads, and I forced my way to the other, climbed over the heap of dead Ylokk, and joined the firing into the crowd of now-confused aliens until it became hard to find a moving target. Someone had closed and barred the gate, so no more were arriving via that route, and the ones inside couldn't get out, but I heard a yell over the din and looked up to see a man fall from a third-story window. It was Borg, the greedy merchant. A Ylokk was looking out the window from which the man had clearly been pushed. I took aim and put a round right between his long, ivory-yellow incisors and he fell back, but was replaced in a moment by two others. They went down in a hail of gunfire from the sergeant's bunch. I nailed the next one. Things began to get quieter, then almost silent. I looked across the hundred-foot-square courtyard and saw no Ylokk on their feet. One, with a yellow stripe on his overcoat, was lying near me, with his eyes open, moaning feebly. He'd been gut-shot. I climbed over to him to put him out of his misery, but he looked around at me and said clearly if squeakily in Swedish:

"Let me save my life and I will give you an empire." Clearly, he'd boned up on our local history: those were Mussolini's last words.

Before I could tell him I didn't need an empire, the red eyes closed and he was dead.

I managed to get the uniformed troops lined up, and assigned them the job of shaping up the civilians. "We have to get through and close the city gate," I told them. "We'll form two squads"—I picked one of my NCOs to lead number two, so as to leave my sergeant in charge in the courtyard— "and advance along the parallel streets to the old city wall. Then we'll move in on the gate."

There were no rat-men in the side streets, and we made our rendezvous with no strife. The gate stood open; it was a rusty wrought-iron affair, intended only as a decorative replacement for the original Medieval oak-plank-and-iron-strap barrier, but it would at least slow an advance.

I did a reconnoiter of the area; no Ylokk in sight. Apparently the ones who had been in the street had retreated. They weren't very enthusiastic warriors. Outside the gate I saw a party of them forming up in a column, no doubt preparing to make use of the treacherously opened gateway. They noticed me closing it, and two started toward me in the unbalanced-looking, slanting-forward, feet-pedaling gait of their kind. It appeared the rodentia hadn't made the transition to upright posture as successfully as the early primates had. They looked like oversized meerkats. Maybe that was why in all our familiar A-lines, Men were in charge while the rats hid and lived on what they could steal from Man's bounty. Anyway, I stepped out to where I had a clear shot, put one over their heads—they still apparently hadn't realized our weapons would kill at a distance—and they went to all fours and ran down a side-alley.

"No guts for the close-in work," my top sergeant, one Per Larsson, commented. "All we got to do," he said, "is to get our manpower organized, and charge. They'll run."

"I hope so," I told him. "Fall 'em in now, Sarge, and try to explain what we have to do."

"We going to take that bunch there?" he asked, sounding a little shocked.

"That very one," I confirmed. "Let's have a twenty-man front, ten deep. Fall in here, outside the gate, make sure your front rank are armed, and the rear ranks, too, as far as our weapons will go. Rear ranks to load and pass weapons forward. We'll start at a walk, laying down aimed fire; when we reach the letter-box there"—I pointed to the blue kiosk with the yellow bugle—"we'll double time. As we take casualties, we'll close up and concentrate our fire on whoever's leading them."

"Yessir," Larsson said, saluted, and took off, yelling orders.

5

My assault force didn't look prepossessing; just a roughly-aligned crowd of the younger, healthier men, and a few tough women, handling their issue revolvers gingerly, as if afraid they'd bite the hand that held them—but willing enough, even eager to go.

I took the pistols away from the two fellows directly behind me and my NCOIC, asked the others to try not to shoot me or Larsson in the back, and gave the order to commence firing and to forward march, hup, two, three, four. They held together pretty well and kept up a lively rate of fire. The Ylokk kept right on with what they were doing until a wild shot hit one of them in the arm. He squealed like a rusty spring and ran—not from us, but from his buddies, who had turned as one to eat him alive. As we got closer, he fell, and the still-healthy ones started to eat. Our fire was hitting targets now. The eaters became the eaten. It was pretty sickening. By the time we reached them, only the dead and dying were left.

"I told you, Colonel," Larsson caroled, "nothing to it!"

"They didn't run, Sarge," I reminded him. "We can't bluff them. And that's hardly the end of it." As I was saying that, a mob of enemy troops debouched from an alley-mouth between two warehouses and came on at a full run. My troops, who had stopped firing, just stood there and watched. Finally Larsson yelled, "Fire at will!"

They laid down an enthusiastic barrage that brought down half the front rank and the mailbox. The rest scattered.

Larsson got busy supervising a redistribution of ammunition, taking rounds from a few fellows who had a pocketful to give to a few complaining shooters who'd used theirs up.

"*Need* about a hundred M-16's here," the sergeant muttered. "But against yellow-bellies like these, I guess our poppers'll do."

"For a while," I agreed. "We need to take a tour around to the other points of entry and give our boys some tips." Larsson saluted and got busy shaping up his crowd of civilians, with the few soldiers as squad leaders. He called the latter "Lieutenant-sir" and saluted them, to give them the needed feeling of authority.

One of them was a kid who looked about sixteen, whom I'd seen before. He was as tall and blond as Swedes are supposed to be, and was a real officer, a First Lieutenant Helm, I found out. He came over to me and tried out a salute. I gave it back to him and took him aside.

"We have to do more than pick them off in small groups, sir," he told me before I could tell him.

"Swell," I agreed. "Let's get to it."

The area immediately outside the restored town wall was given over to small, rustic cottages and their kitchen gardens and outbuildings. Spring in southern Sweden had never been more delightful. There were no rats in sight here; it was hard to realize that strange, alien rat-like invaders were swarming the countryside, killing some people, and making prisoners of others. We saw a few rats skulking in the lee of a barn or stable, but no organized activity. Maybe Richtofen had managed to get things under control back in the capitol, and cut off the enemy reinforcements. I was feeling almost euphoric when I saw the first tank.

It was huge; at first I thought it was a small barn, but then it moved, swaying around to bring a cluster of oversized disruptor cannon to bear on us. I told Helm to take cover, and an instant later a detonation shook the stone walls beside me, and dirt, pebbles, and grit slammed into my back, knocking me down. I rolled to my feet in time to see the clods still falling, along with some bricks from the wall behind me, through a ten-foot gap in which I could see citizens running and others standing in groups, staring toward the hole in the wall. I went through it, yelled to them to run for cover, and went back out to check on the enemy.

The tank, of squat design with a long "front porch" and a railed platform all around, was coming on slowly, rearing up and then dipping its ugly snout as it trampled over stone walls and small buildings. A man ran out to shake a fist at it, and was ignored. The tank approached the wall, ignoring us as it had the other fellow, and stopped.

I called my bunch in and told them to scatter into the woods and find the Major's command post. The hills on the east side of town were heavily wooded. They took off, all but Helm; he stood fast and said, "I guess you might need a little help, Colonel, big as that thing is."

I acknowledged the possibility and wondered what I was going to do next. Just then the lieutenant asked me, "What's your plan, sir?"

"Oh, yes, my plan," I murmured.

My eye fell on a solid-looking fieldstone outhouse a few yards away, behind a modest cottage. The weed crop around it had been mowed short and neat. The enemy tank had stopped near it.

"Lieutenant," I said, "cover me. I'm going to take a look at that mother."

"Now, Colonel," Helm objected. "Why don't I do the snooping while you cover me?"

" 'R,' " I said, " 'H.I.P.' "

He shut up, and held his rifle at the ready. I walked over to the shed, and from its shelter, peeked at the tank, if tank it was; it looked like a battered packing case, but I could just see the caterpillar treads almost buried in the soft turf. There was no sign of life.

I decided to get a closer look. I eased out from the flimsy cover of the privy, feeling like a novice stripper doing her first turn under the baby spots, but keeping both eyes on the tank for signs of activity.

There was nothing until I was within ten feet of it, and could smell the rotten-orange stink of alien coming from it. Then the hatch opened and the pointy snout and narrow shoulders of a Ylokk poked out. He used his stubby arms to hold the cover open while he eased the rest of his overlong torso through. He had a red stripe down the back of his drab overcoat. There were deposits of crusty white stuff around his beady eyes, and foam at the corner of his undershot mouth. He climbed down, moving like an old, old rat, looking for a quiet place to die. He didn't seem to notice me at first, then he did, and turned toward me. His mouth opened, twice; the third time he croaked.

"I call on you to help a fellow-being, slave!" That didn't give me much to go on. He slipped then and fell heavily to the close-cropped turf, and lay, moving aimlessly. I went over, with my automatic in my hand, but I knew I wouldn't need it. I squatted beside him; I could feel the fever from there. The rotten-orange odor was strong on him. He flopped on his back and tried to focus his small red eyes on me.

"Grgsdn was wrong," he croaked. "We have made a dreadful mistake! You are people, like ourselves!"

"Not like yourselves, Rat-face," I said. "Take it easy; I'll see what I can do for you," I added.

He seemed to want to protest, but just gargled and passed out. Helm came over and seemed to want to shoot my prisoner. I told him the fellow was sick and harmless, but he was clearly still itching to shoot the enemy officer anyway. I looked inside the outhouse, just in case he had a friend, and got back out in time to stop Helm. The Ylokk was crawling away from him, repeating *"Jag har inte gjort!"* (I didn't do it!). I called the lieutenant off, and reminded him that our side didn't murder helpless POWs.

"Helpless, hell, sir! Begging your pardon!" Helm burst out. "I've seen the rats swarming into town, eating folks alive!"

"Nevertheless, there's a hospital here," I told him. "And we're going to take this fellow—a general officer, by the way"—I was guessing, but that red stripe meant *some*thing—"over there and see what they can do."

I went back for another look at the abandoned tank. The stink almost got me, but we needed the intelligence. The layout inside was familiar, just like an early-model regulation traveler. That seemed odd. Even the instrument panel looked familiar: the big M-C field-strength meter on the left, the entropic gradient scale to the right, and the temporal matrix gauge dead center. Interesting: it was clearly a rip-off of our own early machines. I climbed down and went back to report what I'd discovered to Helm.

He nodded. "It figures. You wouldn't expect a bunch of rats to develop a technology like that on their own."

"What about their disruptors?" I mentioned. He brushed that off. "Probably stole it from someone else."

We rigged up a stretcher from a ladder and a tarp we found clamped to the side of the tank and got the unconscious Ylokk on it. In the street, we passed a few bold citizens venturing out to see what was happening. They gave our burden a wide berth. At the hospital, we caused quite a stir. The place was packed with citizens, a few with minor injuries from falls and so on, but mostly just seeking reassurance. They reluctantly made way for us, and finally a young internist with "Dr. Smovia" on his nameplate came over and sniffed.

"Smelled that odor on several of these creatures," he commented. "Dead ones. Some epidemic infection, apparently." He cleared some space, called a nurse over to cut off his new patient's garments, revealing a ratty gray pelt, and started his routine of poking and thumping.

"Running ten degrees of fever," he remarked. "Amazing he's still alive. But then, of course, he's *not* human." He called a colleague, took a blood specimen and sent it off to the lab, and gave the general a shot, which seemed to relax him.

"Got to get that fever down," the doc muttered. It was just a technical situation now; he was as intent on his work as if it were the mayor he was working on. He took my protégé away and asked, or rather told, us to wait.

It was half an hour before he came back, looking pleased.

"Virus," he said contentedly. "Working up an anti-viral now. Standard vaccine ought to do it."

Helm and I found a place to wash up, and started looking for some lunch. Smovia hurried off, eager to get back to work.

"No wonder these rats don't show any fight, Colonel," Helm said. "They're sick." He nodded, agreeing with himself.

"Times we saw 'em in heaps," he added. "It explains that. Say, Colonel," he went on, "you s'pose it's like in that book: they caught some kinda disease here they couldn't handle?"

"Nope. I think they were sick when they got here. Maybe that's why they left home. Epidemic."

"Nothing *we* can catch, I hope," Helm commented.

The hospital commissary was closed down, so we went back out in the street and found a hot-dog kiosk and had two each, *med brod och senap* (with bread and mustard). In Sweden you could look on hot dogs bare, if you preferred. Taking our hot dogs we returned to the hospital to find Dr. Smovia looking for me.

He showed me a corked test tube, looking as proud as a new papa. "I've isolated and cultured the virus," he told me. "The contents of this vial," he added, "could fatally infect thousands." He looked uncomfortable. "But of course I shall guard it carefully so as to avoid such a disaster."

"What about the cure?" I prompted.

"Simple enough," he said contentedly. "We can inject the sick, and in a matter of hours they'll be as well as ever."

"We're at war, remember?"

"Of course, Colonel, but to have the power to end an epidemic, and fail to use it . . ." He faded off; apparently he hadn't considered the possibility that I might not be eager to cure the invaders.

"Colonel," he began tentatively, "is there a possibility— If I could go to their home-world, in a matter of hours, the plague would be no more."

"Have you got plenty of that viral culture?" I asked him.

"No, but there's no difficulty in making up as much as needed, now that I know the virus. But why? My vaccine—"

"You're really eager to cure these rats, aren't you Doctor?" I mused aloud.

"Humanitarian considerations," he started. "Of

course we're at war, and must proceed with caution."

"If I can get permission to go to the Ylokk locus," I assured him, "I'll see to it that you come along."

His gratitude was effusive. I cut it off with a question: "You can make up more of the culture, eh? Then you won't mind if I keep this."

"Whatever for?" he responded. "But of course you want a souvenir. Take it and welcome. But *do* exercise care. It's extremely virulent, though not to us, of course, and if it ever accidentally spilled among the Ylokk—"

"I understand," I reassured him. He was so pleased, I didn't have the heart to let him guess I planned to double-cross him. "If you should need me again, Doctor, I'll be at HQ," I added as I turned to leave.

There were dead Ylokk in the street, and the only live ones we saw were running, away from— not after—gangs of armed citizens.

Back at HQ, I used the radio Barbro had found to call GHQ in Stockholm. I got a scared-sounding Lieutenant Sjölund, who told me things were getting out of hand.

"There are just too darn many of them, Colonel! Their casualties are heavy, but they keep on coming! Headquarters is under siege, and so is the Palace and the Riksdag and just about the whole inner city. I don't know how long we can continue resistance. Baron von Richtofen is talking about a counter-attack on their home line, but we really haven't got the trained troops to mount a cross-Net invasion, sir! I'm worried— Hold, sir—"

That was all. Either my radio had packed in, or— I didn't like to think about the "or." If I'd had another few seconds I could have told Sjölund about the vaccine, and how we could use it.

"Too bad, Colonel," Helm agreed. "We have to do something, fast!"

"We will, Lieutenant," I told him. I called Dr. Smovia in, and when he arrived asked him if he was really willing to go on a trip, to help break the near-stalemate.

He was enthusiastic. "But how can we leave here, now?" he wanted to know. "Even if we could get clear of town and through enemy lines, we'd have a long walk to Stockholm."

"We won't be walking," I told him. "Please bring along a field kit you can use to make up more of the viral culture."

"Whatever for?" he wondered aloud. He went off, talking to himself.

"What are we going to do, Colonel?" the lieutenant asked me. "You figuring on trying to bust out of here in one of those school buses you brought in, or what?"

" 'What,' " I told him. "Now, you'd better get on the PA, Helm, and call in all our section leaders." As soon as I heard the crackle of the speakers, I went out into the hall to head for Barbro's office and almost ran into her.

"Just the girl I was looking for," I said, and embraced her warmly, amazed again that this fabulous creature was my wife.

"Why, thank you, Colonel," she replied mockingly. "I thought you'd forgotten about me."

"Not quite," I reassured her. "I'm going to make a little trip, Major, and you'll be in charge here. I want you to fort up here in Headquarters, such as it is: we'll have to do a little ditch-digging and rampart-building, and I want all able-bodied men not assigned to a perimeter position to report here and be prepared for assault."

She looked surprised, an expression as enchanting as all her others.

"Don't worry, they're not on the verge of attacking," I reassured her. "It's just in case. I'm going into the city. I've got information Manfred needs, and *we* need reinforcement. A relatively small, but organized war party from town can take the besiegers on all flanks at once and that'll be that."

6

As soon as my alien guest—oddly, I'd started thinking of him in those terms rather than as my prisoner—was feeling well enough to carry on a coherent conversation, I went in, leaving word with the tough old dame who was the head nurse on the floor that we were not to be disturbed, for anything.

He watched me worriedly with those under-sized red eyes. "You, slave," he said after a while. "I command you to return me to my displacer!"

"Wrong line, Rat-head," I told him. "I'm the one who's healthy and armed and at home. You're the dying stranger. Now, who the hell are you people and what do you want here?"

"I," he began impressively, "am Master General Graf [baron] Swft. I have the honor to command the Second Wave of the Noble Tide. Alas, I am sick. I, who was a champion of one million, I can barely lift my arm! Were it otherwise, I would not now be passively submitting to impudent interrogation! I must resume my command at once!" He made an abortive movement, as if to throw back the blanket, but instead slumped, gnashing those long, yellow incisors.

"Better take it easy, General," I said, in what I meant to be a soothing tone. Instead he lunged at me and snarled. "Do not seek to patronize your betters, vermin!"

"The name's Bayard," I told him. "Colonel Bayard, of the Net Surveillance Service. You're my prisoner of war, and I suggest it would be a good idea to behave yourself. By the way, why are you here?"

"It is the high privilege and manifest destiny of the Noble Folk to occupy and make use of all suitable planes of the multi-ordinal All," he announced. "To this end, I volunteered to conduct a reconnaissance of the Second Devastation—alone, of course, for how could I permit a lesser being to share my high destiny?"

"Alone? There are thousands of you, and more arriving while I sit here and try to figure out what in hell you want."

"On my initial penetration of the Devastation," he explained, "I found a cluster of viable planes of existence deep in the forbidden sector. I reported back to Headquarters and proposed the present mission, under the overall command of Captain General His Imperial Highness the Prince of the Select."

"What is it you want?" I persisted.

"We require this territory as living space for the Noble Folk," he told me, as if belaboring the obvious. "Candidly," he went on, "at my first visit, in an area occupied by a great desert on this plane (it is an inland sea at home), I saw no evidence of life of any kind, and we thought we were occupying a virgin plane. We did not suspect the presence of your own combative kind, akin, we have discovered, to the detestable *yilps*, the ubiquituous primate pests of Ylokk, the scurrying vermin that infest our fruit trees and godowns—as well as garbage dumps," he added, sneering. "And perhaps to their slightly larger jungle-dwelling relatives, the *mongs*. You attacked us on sight; naturally, we responded in kind. You call this 'war' in one of your dialects; we have no word for it. The Noble Folk of Ylokk are peaceful and dwell in amity."

"I've watched some of your 'Noble Folk' eating their dead comrades," I said with audible disapproval. "Sometimes before they were dead. What's noble about that?"

"Ah, my poor fellows are starving," Swft mourned. "At home, we always wait for brain-death before beginning."

"You eat humans, too," I pointed out, "or at least snack a little. We don't like that."

He wagged his narrow head. "Nor do I," he sighed. "It makes one dreadfully bilious. And we're quite sick enough already. The disease, in truth, is what drove us here."

"Aha! The truth at last."

"I have spoken truly," the alien huffed. "In Great Ylokk, the disease rages, killing whole towns; our civilization is crumbling! Cities are become charnel houses, where looters roam, attacking the helpless! You, as a sentient being, must, of course do all you can to alleviate suffering on such a scale!"

"Our altruism doesn't extend, quite, to allowing you to take over *our* world and destroy *our* culture," I explained. "You'll have to call it off, General, and find another solution. Try Sector Thirty-five. There's a fine swath of unoccupied Lines there, where, as far as we can determine, the mammals didn't make it, and the insects rule the world."

"Pah!" he spat. "You'd relegate the Noble Folk to a nest of fleas? You will regret this insolence, Colonel!"

"I doubt it, General," I told him. "But it isn't my feelings—or yours—that are the problem we're facing. The problem is how I can convince you this invasion of yours won't work, before we've both suffered irreparable damage?"

"Your word 'invasion,' implying as it does the violent seizure of territory rightfully the property of others, is inappropriate," he snarled. "We found no population of the Noble Folk here, and never dreamed of the existence of another sapient species —especially an overgrown yilp or mong. We came as peaceful colonists to people a deserted world."

"You must have realized your mistake pretty quickly," I pointed out. "You couldn't have imagined the buildings and machines you encountered were natural formations."

"You mongs—" he stated.

" 'Humans,' " I corrected.

"Very well, 'humongs,' if it matters," he resumed impatiently, "and we Ylokk as well, are a part of nature, and all our works are natural. As natural, say, as a bird's nest, or a beehive, a beaver dam, a larva's labyrinth, a spider's web, and so on. I concede I had doubts when I saw what was clearly a city, if overly spacious and light-drenched."

"That's the first time anybody ever described Stockholm in those terms," I commented. "Why didn't you call it off when you saw we were civilized? You can drop the pretense that you didn't know: your points of entry are all located in major cities."

He waved that away, weakly. "The proper sites for cities," he said didactically, "are constant across the planes. We quite naturally sited our staging depots in our cities; thus we arrived in yours."

"What about the first time?" I chivvied him, "when you say you arrived in a desert?"

"An experimental displacer installation, located on a tiny island in the Sea of Desolation, for reasons of security," he grumped.

"You should have backed off as soon as you saw the first town," I insisted.

"Impossible!" the sick alien croaked. "The plan was too far advanced in execution—and the need to escape disease remained!"

"Why didn't you develop a vaccine against this disease?" I wanted to know.

He looked bewildered. "I recall the word, of course," he said. "My deep briefing was complete, if hurried. But the concept eludes me: to interfere, by one's own actions, with a Provision of Nature? Our philosophers have perceived that the Killing is in fact, a benign dispensation of Nature to alleviate the problem of overpopulation. You would propose to interfere with the working of the Will?"

"In a small way," I conceded. "This disease of yours is caused by a virus, a competing life-form, which invades your tissues, destroys red blood cells, gives you headaches, weakens you, and finally kills you. It doesn't have to. It can be cured."

"You rave, Colonel," he countered. "Surely you don't believe it's possible to influence the workings of the Will?"

"We do it all the time," I told him. "It's part of the Will; that's what this building is for. Why do you think we brought you here?"

"To kill me, of course," he supplied promptly. "Debased creatures though you are, you could not fail to recognize in me a superior being, and are according me a high ritual death suitable to my rank. I acknowledge your propriety in this matter, at least. I await the moment of awful truth unflinchingly. Bring on your shamans! Do your worst! I shall die as a peer of the Noble Folk should!"

"We're trying to cure you, not kill you, General," I told him, feeling weary. I had a right to feel weary. I hadn't slept since . . . I couldn't remember.

"I call on you now to place a sword in my hand," he declared as if he fully expected instant obedience. "My own hallowed blade is in my displacer. Fetch it at once!"

"If you're so peaceful," I said, "what's all this 'hallowed blade' stuff? A pig-sticker is a pig-sticker, isn't it?"

"Your astounding ignorance is beneath my contempt," he told me. "The origins of the Code of Honor lie so far back in the history of the Noble Folk that—but I perceive you mock me," he changed the tack. "You yourself are no stranger to the Code of the Warrior—or your distorted version of it."

I let that one pass. "So you have no medical science whatever?" I mused aloud. "With your obvious high technology in other areas, one would expect—"

"Pah!" he squeaked. "As well to demand a science of weather control. Doubtless you've noted that across all the phases, or A-lines as you say, the weather is unchanging."

I agreed I'd noticed that.

"Even here, so far outside the formal limits of the Governance," he added. "The sole exceptions are the areas of the Devastations, where the very landforms have been disrupted, modifying the air and water currents."

"And you crossed the Blight, or Devastation if you prefer, to seek out our phase, above all others," I stated. "Why? Why not some closer line, one more like your own home-worlds? And what do you mean, 'Devastations'? There's only one Blight."

"At the fringes of our jurisdiction," Swft told me, readily enough, "we found repeated evidence of the presence of a rival power—your own, I now perceive. By mathematical methods, we deduced the focal point of this interference—the Other Devastation. We already knew, of course, of the strange Devastation surrounding our own home-phase. When I explored here in this second Devastation, I had no reason to expect to encounter rational beings. We assumed your nexus had perished in the terrible upheaval that created your 'Blight.'"

"Your 'Devastation,'" I told him, "is no doubt the result of failed displacer experiments in the closely allied lines. You should have realized that a second such area of destruction indicated another Net-traveling line. But you just started in to claim some vacant real estate," I finished sarcastically.

"Once our enterprise was launched," he told me as if stating the obvious, "using, as it had, the last of our resources, there was no turning back. Can you imagine me, the originator of the scheme, returning to Ylokk mere days after our gala embarkation, to report to the Noblest of All that it had turned out to be inconvenient to pursue the plan further?"

"Awkward," I agreed. "But you'll have to do it anyway. You've seen enough to realize you can't make it stick."

"Perhaps," he remarked. "Perhaps not as originally conceived, but there are other approaches, more subtle ones, that might yet prevail. Not all your local phases are as well-organized and informed as this, your Zero-zero coordinate."

"You're talking yourself into a short life stretch in solitary," I warned him. "All this is being recorded, of course, and there are those in the Imperial government who would be extremely cautious about releasing an agent of the enemy to continue activities prejudicial to the peace and order of the Imperium. We, too, have noticed traces of Net operations—yours, I presume—beyond the edge of our Zone of Primary Interest. We had planned some day to trace you to your source, and . . ." I broke off, thinking suddenly of a bleak region we called Zone Yellow.

"And invade *us*," the alien supplied.

"The idea of a preemptive strike had been mentioned," I had to concede. "But we hoped to establish a cooperative relationship, as we have with still other Net powers."

"I fear the carnage here obviates that possibility," he declared. "Both from our viewpoint and your own. Unfortunate, perhaps. But, to be candid, I doubt our people would ever have been able to overcome their instinctive distaste for the mong tribe."

"You and I seem to be doing all right," I pointed out. "I hardly ever think of you in terms of bristly sewer rats anymore."

"I've had the opportunity to read in your literature, during a null-time TDY," the alien general told me. "I was revolted by the cruel treatment you have accorded the distant relatives of the Noble Folk. But I confess our own persecution of the vile yilps has been no less genocidal."

"Maybe we've both made mistakes," I suggested. "But right now, the problem is that your people are still pouring in here at the rate of over a million a day."

"Three million," he corrected crisply. "Our overcrowding is acute," he added in explanation.

"Not via the staging depot on Strandvägen," I challenged. "We've monitored it long enough to know."

"There are eleven major mass-transfer portals," he told me, "including a few in truly deserted areas. The one you know and are doubtless prepared to destroy with your curious active-at-a-distance projectile weapons, was the first. We realized we'd erred in imagining the phase to be uninhabited, and placed others in areas remote from your population centers."

"Not quite," I corrected. "Your troops have been reported from all major capitals. You're not warlike, but you started a war," I summed up wearily. "You wouldn't think of invading the territory of a sentient species, but here you are. Your story lacks credibility, General."

He wagged his narrow head, a gesture of assent

he'd apparently picked up from us humans, and said, "I can readily understand your confusion, Colonel. But it is not enough merely to identify apparent inconsistencies in my account of affairs. You *must*," he was very serious now, "*must* understand this much: the needs of the Noble Race are paramount. Your feckless resistance to our peaceful occupation of needed living space must cease at once! It is an inconvenience not to be borne!"

"You were doing the 'reasonable' number, remember, General?" I countered. "What about *our* living space? And after all, we humongs *are* the rightful owners of the territory in question."

"By *what* right?" he came back, as if he'd been hoping I'd say that.

"By right of birth, prior occupation and development, and human need," I told him, as if *I'd* been waiting for the question.

" 'Prior occupation . . .' " he mused. "I think your local 'rats,' as you call these humble folk, have at least as ancient a claim."

"Not to our granaries!" I told him; I was beginning to get a little impatient with his bland absurdities.

"How not?" he riposted. "The produce of the soil knows no 'natural' exploiter. The plants grow for whoever can reap them."

"We plant them," I told him, "and reap them, too. We built our cities and stocked them, and that's too obvious to talk about!"

He gave me an oblique look. "You 'planted' them, you say. I fear we're entering an area touched on only lightly in my autobriefing—another curious concept, implying manipulation of the Will."

"You're telling me you don't practice agriculture?" I queried incredulously.

He hesitated before replying. "I know the term, of course, but fail to comprehend it. 'To cause plants to grow in concentration in a specified area.' It is beyond belief. Plants grow where they will."

I talked to him for another half hour, without any notable progress. He still held to the view that humanity ought to get out of the way of the Noble Folk, thereby ending hostilities.

"You claim you know nothing of us," I reminded him, "and yet you arrived here fully briefed and with command of both Swedish and English. How do you explain that?"

"I am," he replied stiffly, "under no compulsion to explain anything. However," he continued, "I see no harm to my cause in clarifying what I perceive must seem mysterious to you. Very well:

"We have developed a technique of rapid transfer of information to deep memory, a development, actually, of the ancestral ability to remember the location of buried nuts. My discovery-contact with your plane gave, as I've explained, no indication of habitation, since I arrived, as we now know, in a great desert—the 'Sahara,' I've learned you call it. At home the site is that of a shallow sea. The subsequent routine follow-up crews, however, found primitive temporary camps of your kind, those of nomadic tribes, it developed; so naturally the follow-up teams went on to scout more widely. It was they who assembled the briefing materials, with the exception of the linguistic data on the two related dialects extant here at my designated point of entry, which coincides, of course, with the position of the Noble City. Those last data were, of course, hastily gathered at the last moment before our scheduled jump-off; hence the imperfections in my command of the tongues."

"You're doing fine," I encouraged him.

He gave me a haughtily defensive look, if I could read the limited range of expression on his snouted face. "We erred," he intoned, "in not more thoroughly examining our target plane. But you must recall: we were—and are—in a desperate situation, and time was of the essence. A less sensitive people, such as yourselves, would have simply thrown in an overwhelming force, without consideration of possible consequences for the indignies."

"Gosh," I said. "Maybe we all ought to just whisk ourselves off into the Blight."

"Nothing so drastic," he corrected. "A mass evacuation to one of the Blight Insulars would be quite adequate. We will permit and even expedite such an accommodation. I can go so far as to say that we will place at your disposal our method of mass-transfer."

"I was kidding," I explained. Then I had to explain what "kidding" was. "We have no intention of abandoning our homeland," I summed up.

"In that case," he said in a tone of forced patience, "I can see no prospect of any peaceful accommodation between our two species. Pity. Together we might have accomplished much."

"We still have a lot of talking to do, General," I told him. "I'd better go now. You get some rest; I'll see you tomorrow."

"Speaking with you, Colonel," he answered, "I had for a moment almost forgotten the desperate plight of the Folk. Fare well."

On that note, I left him and his lingering odor of rotten oranges. For a moment there it had seemed possible that we could somehow reconcile our disparate interests, something that would be of great benefit to both species: the Ylokk had some techniques the NSS would find very useful, and again there was a lot we could teach them, too; but now I was feeling very low. I wanted to talk to Barbro: just the sound of her voice would cheer me up, but what I had to tell her—that I had to make a dash for Headquarters to report what I'd learned about the invaders (and I'd learned more than Swft knew he'd told me)—wouldn't cheer *her* up.

I found her, as usual, in the thick of the hottest crisis we had going: a breakthrough had penetrated our improvised defenses on the river side of town. She was at Field HQ, monitoring the situation map with its cheery (if you didn't know what they meant) colored lights indicating the position of the enemy, unit-by-unit; as they advanced raggedly out of the forest, and of our inadequate forces as they held and held—and fell back. In a few minutes, it appeared, the hospital would be surrounded and isolated.

"Fortunately, Brion," she reported to me, "we are perhaps saved by the fact that they are making even more and worse mistakes than we."

I was giving her a fast briefing when Dr. Smovia came hurrying up to me, trailed by a sheepish female MP. I waved her off, and asked Barbro to carry on. Then I kissed her good-bye for now. Smovia was hovering, looking worried.

"Look here, Colonel," he carped, "my patient is *hardly* ready to leave the hospital. In addition, he's a carrier—"

"No danger to humans, though?" I said hopefully.

"Of course not," he brushed that aside. "But it *is* rather high-handed of you to release him without so much as notifying me—"

"Hold it," I cut in. "I haven't released him! I left him in bed ten minutes ago! Do you mean—?"

"He's gone," Smovia grumped. "Not in the hospital. I've checked. I assumed that you—"

I cut him off. "He's on his own, I'm afraid." I went to the window and looked down the street. As I'd feared, the alien traveler wasn't where I'd left it, unguarded. Barbro patted my arm encouragingly. She knew I was mentally kicking myself.

"Get on the hot line, Barb," I told her. "Tip off our perimeter stations to be on the lookout—but don't try to stop him. They can't; it would just give us needless casualties."

"What does this mean?" Smovia demanded. "Where would he go, still weak as he is?"

"Home," I told him curtly. "He's gone now; it can't be helped." I turned to Barbro. "This makes my dash for the city more necessary than ever," I told her. She understood that, and nodded. I took off. I couldn't find my sergeant; I left word for him and went out into the street, where I flagged down Lieutenant Helm and told him I was going to break out. He naturally wanted more details, and I told him to round up the best of our three half-tracks and meet me on Kungsgatan in half an hour. He left at a run.

I went back inside and found Smovia and asked him to come along, and to bring his alien virus cultures. He didn't understand why, but didn't give me an argument. I got our HQ crew busy digging defensive works, and briefed them.

"I'll be back in forty-eight hours," I told them. "Hold your position until then." They said they could, and would. I hoped so. Lieutenant Helm returned with the tracks gassed, provisioned, and ready. We didn't bother with subtleties; we went out the gate past where I'd carelessly left Swft's displacer unguarded, and saw the same disorganized skirmishers with their short-range weapons. I could almost believe Swft's contention that the Ylokk weren't warlike. They made no attempt to interfere; then we came to the roadblock. It was a forbidding-looking barrier at first glance: felled trees, interlaced, with the interstices stacked full of rubble. I took to the shoulder and went across some bumpy ground and back onto the undamaged road. A few Ylokk ran in toward us, but halted at a distance. For invaders, they didn't seem to have much idea what they were doing.

"Don't underrate them," I advised Helm. "They have some technology and ought to be capable of waging effective warfare even without military science. But as individuals they seem to have no imagination or initiative. If we do anything unexpected, they're at a loss."

"Suppose it occurs to one of them to get in our path and fire a disruptor at close range?" he mused aloud.

"In that case, we shoot him, proving it was a bad idea," I replied. But I was worried. We kept on, and they let us through. After a few miles we didn't see any more of the skulking rat-men. It was an hour's run to the suburbs. We came to the first bridge into Stockholm and it was intact. Five minutes later we were moving along Drottningatan unimpeded. There were heaps of dead aliens in the streets, along with a few human bodies, attended only by scavenging Ylokk. The air filters kept the worst of the stink out of the truck's cab.

In spite of their massive casualties, there were still plenty of the rat-men abroad, marching in ragged columns, mostly along narrow back streets, sometimes herding human captives. There was no visible damage to the city. The lone shot I'd seen fired in Strandvägen was unique. We came to the high wrought-iron fence in front of Headquarters and were met and escorted inside by two snappy officers in Swedish field-gray.

7

Manfred von Richtofen leaned across his big desk to shake my hand warmly, after he'd returned Helm's salute. I introduced Dr. Smovia, who gave Manfred a terse briefing on his findings, then went off to cook up more viral culture.

"A vaccine, you say?" Richtofen inquired dubiously. "What— ?"

"These creatures are swarming in here faster than our forces and the disease combined can kill them, sir," I pointed out. "We can't stay strictly on the defensive; we have to counter-attack."

Manfred nodded doubtfully. "We've traced their C.H. date," he told us. "Over one hundred million years, Brion, and in Zone Yellow at that."

We both turned to look at the Net map that covered one wall. It showed the large irregularly-shaped cross-section of A-lines so far explored by the Imperium, with an overlaid grid, and a blue line outlining the area in which the Imperial government claimed sovereignty. At dead center, the Zero-zero line—the home-world—was indicated by a scarlet dot. Nearby were three more red dots, all included within the big pink blotch of the Blight—the area of desolate, abnormal world-lines overwhelmed by the runaway entropic energies disastrously released by the near-analogs there of Maxoni and Cocini, whose work had succeeded only here, and had been guided past catastrophe only here and in the three Blight Insular Lines.

I knew little about Zone Yellow, a second area of ruined A-lines, analogous to the Blight, but not associated with it, except for the news that it was Ylokk home-area.

"Sir," I offered, "we have to hit back."

Manfred looked at me grimly. "We've surrounded their main point of entry," he said as if I hadn't spoken. "The warehouse off Strandvägen. I'm planning a raid, and—"

"No mass attack is necessary, sir. When I dump this vial in their water supply—"

It was his turn to butt in. "I—I cannot in conscience dispatch a lone man into an interdicted and totally unknown region of the Net, Brion. Especially my most valued and experienced officer. No, I need you here."

I was drawing a breath to rebut that when the roof fell in, quite literally. A chunk of concrete the size of a pool table smashed Richtofen's desk flat, knocking him back in a cloud of plaster dust. Ripped-loose wiring sparked and cracked, and in a few seconds, fire was flickering among the dumped papers from a burst filing cabinet. Helm grabbed my arm and pulled me back. I hurriedly told him I was all right—and I was, except for the ringing in my ears and some choking dust in my lungs. He found Smovia, dazed, slumped in a corner, and got him on his feet. I went back into the smoke and hauled Manfred out. He was semi-conscious, but not hurt.

"It appears," he said when he'd caught his breath, "that our decision is academic. If they've brought up their big guns—their disruptors can easily be built to any size desired—we needn't concern ourselves with counterattack. We'll have our hands full surviving."

There were people in the room by then, yelling conflicting orders at each other. I got the attention of a senior colonel and suggested he try to get everybody to calm down and wait for orders. While I was telling him this, he was telling me that the blast had been due to a low-flying aircraft of alien design, an ornithopter like a giant dragonfly.

Manfred was dusty, but unhurt. He said, "Dismissed!" and the mob went silent and disappeared.

"I'll get in there, sir," I assured him. "All I have to do is watch the instruments."

"I don't like it," Richtofen grumped. "It's been twenty years since we so much as conducted a reconnaissance at such a distance, and as you well know, it came to grief. No, Zone Yellow is off limits. The technical people aren't sure we can penetrate it, and once in, there can be no return: the entropic gradient is too steep. Any plan to counterattack is, all too apparently, impractical. Accordingly, we must wage the war here, on our own territory."

"I studied one of the Ylokk machines," I told him. "There are a couple of tricks we can employ. I'd like permission to modify a three-man scout and give it a try."

Manfred nodded absently, "The warehouse we've surrounded . . ." It was as if he hadn't heard a word I'd said.

"Excuse me, General, I think we have to tackle this thing at its source. I can make it work—"

"No, Brion. I cannot allow this. No, I need you here. *We* need you here. Barbro, waiting at Sigtuna—who knows what may have befallen her by now? No, no," he reversed field. "No doubt she and her people are holding their own . . ."

"All the more reason I have to *do* something, sir," I insisted. All of a sudden I was eager to get going. "I can draw equipment and be on the way in half an hour."

"Not alone!" Richtofen snapped.

"I seem to recall, sir," I countered, "in the old days you did your best work when you were alone."

"I was young and foolish," he grumped. "My flying circus was superb! I suppose I liked to roam the skies over France apart from the Staffel partly from egoistic impulses: Alone, the victory was indisputably mine!"

"*This* isn't an ego trip, General," I assured him.

"Then why do you propose to go alone?"

"Not quite alone, sir," I put in. "I need Dr. Smovia and Lieutenant Helm."

"Little enough help in an emergency," Manfred snapped.

"I want to be inconspicuous," I reminded him. "The idea is to sneak in, dump the virus culture in their water supply, and duck back out."

"In Zone Yellow, Brion?" He pressed the point. "You're as aware as I that the entropic gradient at such a distance is insurmountable!"

"Theory, sir," I rebutted. "I think it can be done. I'll need to watch my latent-temporal drain very closely, and keep the entropic gradient in the green."

After a thoughtful pause, the General made a gesture of resignation. "I see you've set your mind on this mad escapade, my friend," he conceded. "Think of all you'll be risking."

"Don't talk me out of it, sir," I pled. "I'm not really happy about it—it's just that it has to be done."

He literally threw up his hands. "Very well, then, Colonel. You'll have the best equipment we have. I'll call Sjölund." He did so.

I got Manfred out of the building and into his big Saab limo, where his driver, a spidery little fellow named Ole (pronounced oo-luh) was waiting, ignoring the panic all around him. I got in front.

"Drive me to Strandvägen, Ole," Richtofen directed him. The big car oozed along the bumpy cobbled street like syrup flowing over waffles, and we pulled up in front of the big, glitzy Intercontinental Hotel, formerly an abandoned ship's chandler's warehouse. Security men were ten deep around it, but they waved their boss through with no delay.

"There's a brick vault under the building," he told me. "Dates back to the sixteenth century. Very stable. They've taken it over as their staging depot. They're bringing in troops in battalion lots at six-hour intervals. Easy target, except for the jet-set tenants directly above. They haven't been bothered, except for some nightmares, it seems. Leakage from the Ylokk version of the M-C drive."

"Too bad," I commented. "We can't have our telly stars and playboys dreaming they had to go to work."

"It's no joke, Brion," Manfred reprimanded me. "General von Horst lives there, and so does Crmblnski, the chap who developed the Holautosome, you know. Very popular fellow. Could hardly ask him to move out so we could blow up his art collection."

"That 'holauto' gadget is the one that lets you control and record REM dreams, isn't it?"

"Precisely; the opiate of the masses," Richtofen replied without approval. "As you know, it's made Crmblnski a popular hero."

"We'd better evacuate them anyway," I commented.

Manfred shook his head. "Some of these people have spent millions of kronor and half their lives in assembling collections of bric-a-brac and evolving a suitable environment for showing it off—except that nobody's allowed to see them. We'd have to evict them forcibly."

I looked at him to see if he was joking. He wasn't.

"We'd better start now, General," I told him. "Look! Here comes another batch of reinforcements." A column of ten rats abreast was filing out of the old loading shed, cleaner and snappier than the ones I'd seen, and ready to take on a world—*our* world.

"We can't keep on stacking corpses forever, General," I pointed out. A few shouts rang out and rat-men fell out of ranks, formed up in a column of twos, and headed off down the street. They made no attempt to assume an offensive formation, or even a defensive one; just marched as if they were on a parade ground. Maybe they were; a strange heavy vehicle with a staff-car look had eased around the corner and pulled up by the shed.

"There's our target, General," I said, and started to get out of the car.

Richtofen waved me back as he spoke into his talker. "One round from the eighty-eight, Colonel," he directed crisply. "I want a direct hit," he added. "There's no room for a ranging shot."

"Can't have the people upstairs getting the idea there's a war on," I agreed. The shot was fired, and the car was enveloped in a raging ball of dust, which blew away to reveal the vehicle, apparently unharmed.

"You see our problem, Colonel," Richtofen said. "It appears they've responded to our high explosives and projectiles by developing a variation of the disruptor principle to contain and absorb explosions. Incredibly fast work! We're facing a formidable foe, make no mistake, Colonel!"

This was getting serious. He'd called me "Colonel" twice in one breath. He called me by my rank only when things were really sticky.

"Suppose I sneak up and let the air out of their tires," I suggested in a mock-conspiratorial tone, but Manfred was in no mood for my sense of humor. Neither was I. Of course, I had already reported the tank-traveler I'd briefly captured; we were surprised we hadn't seen more. There were only the foot soldiers, but there were a lot of them. Someone had said three million: Intelligence had upped its estimate to four million, in Stockholm and elsewhere, give or take a few hundred thousand, with more arriving every second.

"We're losing ground fast." Manfred smacked his palm with his fist. "We need to *do* something, dammit!" Actually, he said "devil" or its Swedish equivalent, which is as close as the Swedish language can come to swearing. He seldom spoke

German; he'd been here ever since his forced landing in 1917. He gave me an angry look and said, "No, Brion; I can see no alternative at the moment. But surely a large unit capable of carrying a ten-man strike team would be best."

"Sorry to disagree, sir," I said. "I don't want to go out in a blaze of glory attempting the impossible: challenging a nation with a handful of suicide-squaders. I want to slip in with no fanfare and do what needs to be done. According to this Swft, they're in desperate condition already. What I have in mind—"

"Very well," Richtofen cut me off. "As you wish, but I'm doubtful—*very* doubtful—that your approach will succeed. Instead, I fear I'll simply lose my best officer."

"Plus a couple of other fellows," I said.

I sent Helm off to requisition some issue rations, and get back ten minutes ago.

He took off at a run, and I got back down to business. There was no time to waste. Dr. Smovia had gone off to talk to our medical people.

"Manfred, if I don't make it, I know you'll see to it that Barbro is well taken care of." He nodded gruffly, and on that note we went to the Net garages.

The former car barn near Stallmästaregården still looked like a car barn; even the streetcar tracks were still in place, used for moving cargo carts. The original old-fashioned gold and blue streetcars had been shipped to Lima, Peru, years ago. I hoped they were well taken care of. There was a neat brick walk beside a trimmed hedge leading to the personnel door under a row of linden trees. We went back.

It was a big, echoey space, with little office-cubicles along one side, and half a dozen shuttles of various shapes and sizes parked across the orange-painted floor with a ruled three-foot grid of white lines, helpful in pinpointing positions of the vehicles when it was necessary to shift into tight quarters at the destination.

We stood for a moment just inside the personnel entry, and looked at the technical people swarming over, under, and around the travelers, some with a plain packing-crate look, others disguised as heavy trucks or buses, two or three gotten up in heavy war-hulls that looked like what they were: our latest Mark XX all-terrain tanks, with enough armament to blast their way out of any situation.

"A Mark III, I think," Manfred said as if suggesting it.

I shook my head, though he wasn't looking at me. "My idea, sir," I said, trying not to sound dogged, "is to sneak in there unnoticed and work quietly."

He nodded. "As you wish, Brion. Personally, I don't think anything you, a single man, can do will bring to heel a nation of invaders whose own world is in a state of chaos, judging from your report."

"Maybe it won't work," it was my turn to concede, "but maybe it will. Raw force won't. And I won't be *quite* alone; Lieutenant Helm and Doctor Smovia will be with me."

Sjölund and a bunch of technicians were in a huddle around an innocuous-looking lift-van, a wooden crate stout enough to be hoisted, fully loaded, aboard ship without collapsing. I went over. A young fellow named Rolf saw us first and came to attention.

"Zone Yellow, eh, sir?" he queried, but not as though he didn't know the answer. I looked inside the van. It would be cramped for three, but it would do.

"They volunteered?" Manfred inquired punctiliously. I nodded. I hadn't given them much of a chance not to, but if they didn't want to go, all they had to do was get accidently delayed in their errands. Helm was as gung ho as they came; I wasn't worried about that. As for Smovia, he was so wrapped up in the medical ramifications, he wouldn't notice where he was.

8

I spent a few minutes warming up the M-C drive, and running through a routine pre-trip; everything was in the green. It had been a while, so I tried a little experimenting, just to get the feel of the controls again, shifting a few A-lines, within the B-1-one parameters, of course, avoiding the Blight, though I did dip in long enough to fix a view on the screen of a line that was as bad as any I'd ever looked at on my previous fast trips across the Blight. It was horrible. The trick was to come close enough to the blighted A-line to see detail without dropping into identity with it, a fate too dismal to contemplate.

Helm arrived with his supplies, breathing hard: he'd had a run-in with a squad of Ylokk. We stowed the stuff aft; when we came back out to the front compartment, he recoiled at what he saw on the screen: a vast green and yellow jungle overgrowing the ruins of buildings, with immense worms that were actually free-living human intestines writhing over the matted foliage.

"What's *that*?" he blurted.

I spent a few minutes trying to explain it to him, actually stalling, waiting for Smovia to come back. Manfred was at the door of the van, watching for his arrival—he'd sent a man to find him and hurry him up. He looked at the big wall clock at one-minute intervals. Finally Smovia arrived at a dead run. "See here, Colonel . . ." he started.

Just then there was a detonation from the direction of the main cargo doors, one of which slammed into view, crumpled like scrap paper. A crowd of Ylokk were right behind it. Shots were fired, and rats fell, kicking. I grabbed Smovia's arm and urged him into the disguised shuttle, then picked off an eager rat who was too close to ignore. Then, after Helm got back in, I stepped into the cramped compartment and clamped the hatch behind me. Somebody was pounding on the hull. We had to go.

Helm had gone back to watching the horrors on the screen: a vast heap of pale-veined flesh now, with human limbs and heads growing from it like warts. He wanted to know how such monstrosities could be.

I tried to explain. Like most Swedes, and most other people as well, he had heard only vague rumors of the Imperium and the vast skein of alternate-probability worlds over which the Net Monitor Service maintained an ongoing surveillance, not interfering with the unfolding of events except in case of imminent threat to the Imperium itself, or to the integrity of the whole manifold. We weren't alone in this endeavor; a humanoid

species called the Xonijeel maintained their own
Interdimensional Monitor Service, attempting, like
us, to prevent any further catastrophe such as the
one that had precipitated the area of runaway en-
tropy, the swatch of ruined A-lines surrounding
the Zero-zero line—a disaster Xonijeel had avoided
more by luck than any particular countermeasures.
Agent Dzok of Xonijeel called our Zero-zero line
B-1-one, and by avoiding the Blight, they had
missed us for a century.

"There are a few other Net-traveling peoples," I
told Helm, "including some you wouldn't want to
meet in a dark alley. The Haqqua, for example—C.H.
date about one hundred thousand BP—and now,
it seems, the Ylokk, from a lot farther away. In fact
we've never successfully carried out a reconnaissance that far out."

I pointed out to Helm the curious phenomenon
of E-entropy: the gradual changes as we sped
across the lines of alternate reality, analogous to
the changes we observe as we move unidirection-
ally in time. The looming mass of the Net garage
had changed as we watched the screen; the color
went from the dull gray PVC of the paneled walls
to a blotchy greenish-yellow; cracks appeared,
patches curled and fell away, revealing a red-oxide
steel-truss structure beneath. This slowly modified
into rusting, sagging scrap-iron, and at last fell
among the rank weed-trees that had been unobtrusively growing into a veritable jungle. After half
an hour, only a slight mound, tree-covered, marked
the spot.

That didn't seem to make the lieutenant, or me
either, feel a lot better. But we sped along at a
thousand A-lines per minute across the Blight and
into more normal-looking territory. As soon as we

were clear, I adjusted course, and in a few minutes we were in Zone Yellow, with no unusual phenomena, so far.

As always, it was fascinating. Today, I looked out at glistening mud-flats that rose barely above the choppy surface of the sea that stretched to the horizon. The weather, of course, was the same as it had been: a bright, sunny morning with a few fleechy clouds. One of them, I thought, looked like a big fish eating a smaller one. It was a curious thing: in the areas of the Net distant from the Zero-zero line, one never saw human faces in the cloud-patterns, or even normal, familiar animals. These fish I was seeing in the mist were monstrous, all jaws and spines. So much for fanciful ideas; we had places that wanted us to go to them, and things itching to be done. After a while, the sea drained away and vegetation appeared; tall, celery-like trees, which were quickly covered by a tide of green, as others sprouted and grew tall.

As we rushed on, E-velocity being our only defense against falling into identity with the desolation around us, we watched the trees wither, as great vines suffocated them. The vines became a web of what looked like electric distribution cables. A mound where the garages had been burst and spilled forth strange, darting vehicles, and monstrous caricatures of men, rendered hideous by gross birth defects and mutations. They scurried among the dead trees along well-trodden paths that writhed, changing course like water spilling down an uneven slope. Abruptly there was a blinding flash of white light, a flash that burned on and on, dazzling our eyes until the overload protection tripped and the screen faded, but not quite to total darkness; we could see a dim landscape under a bloated red moon. Low mounds dotted the exposed rock to the edge of a dark sea. What had once been Stockholm, and on its own plane of alternate existence still was, had been inundated by the Baltic Sea. Just at the edge of the water, partially submerged, was a giant crater, a good half-mile wide. The brilliant light we had seen had been a house-sized meteorite, which had dealt the final blow to the degenerate remnants of animal life in this doomed area of the Blight.

"My God," Helm blurted. "Is it all like this?"

"Happily, no," I told him. "But some of it's worse. We're into Zone Yellow now—you've seen it on the Net map back at HQ. The Common History dates of the closest lines beyond the Blight are a few thousand years BP. This is perhaps a few million. The forces Cocini and Maxoni were meddling with when they developed the M-C drive that powers our Net travelers were potent entropic energies. They were lucky; they contained the forces and succeeded in giving us access to the entire Net of alternate possibilities. Other experimenters, the analogs of Maxoni and Cocini in their own lines, were not so lucky. Our own line was the survivor; all the very close A-lines were destroyed, with the exception of a couple where Cocini and Maxoni never started their work."

"You told me about a couple of lines you'd visited where things are pretty normal," Helm commented. "How——?"

"A few other lines within the blighted area survived," I repeated. "Because there Maxoni and Cocini never met—or never started their work. Those are the Blight Insulars."

Helm nodded like a man resigned to not understanding.

On the screen, the view now was again of an expanse of glistening sea-mud; the sea had once more receded, leaving sodden flats that stretched to the horizon. We saw no sign of life here, except the scattered skeletons of whales and of a few large fish, plus a fascinating assortment of sunken ships, which ranged from the ribs of Viking dragon-ships to eighth-of-a-mile-long submarine cargo vessels of the latest model. The drained area went on for a long time. I was getting sleepy.

I checked over the instruments and controls again and explained them to Helm—"Just in case," I pointed out over his objections, "it becomes convenient for you to operate this thing." As soon as he quit protesting, he turned out to be a quick study. He pointed to the SUSTAIN gauge and said, "If this starts down, I have to turn the BOOST knob to the right, eh?"

"Right," I agreed. "Just a little." I didn't mention that too much gain would send us into entropic stasis, stuck.

At last, the scene outside began gradually to change. First the crater walls in the background collapsed and were covered by vegetation that foamed up like a green tide that rose in tall, conical evergreen breakers. Long, pinkish-purple worms appeared, twining through the lush greenery, leaving stripped limbs, boughs and twigs in their wake. When they met, they intertwined, whether in battle or copulation I couldn't tell. At last the worms dwindled and were no bigger than garden snakes, and as agile. But not agile enough to escape a quick-pouncing feathered thing like a fluffy frog that dropped on worm after worm, consumed them in a gulp, and leapt again. They swarmed; the glimpses of worm became less frequent and at last there was only the stripped and rotting forest, clotted with shaggy nests of twigs, and frog-birds in various sizes, the larger eating the smaller, as eagerly as their ancestors had eaten worms. It was difficult to maintain the realization that I wasn't traveling across time, but perpendicular to it, glimpsing successive alternate realities, as close-related worlds evolved at rates proportional to their displacement from the key line of their group.

A tiny, darting mammal appeared, sharp-nosed and small-eyed, peeping over the edge of a big, ragged nest full of glistening gray eggs the size of golf balls. There was yolk on its snout.

"A rat!" Helm blurted. "We must be on the right track, sir! Congratulations!"

"Don't celebrate yet, Andy," I suggested, though I felt as pleased as he sounded. We watched the tiny rodent-like animals; soon they became bigger, less agile, using their forelegs for grasping as they leaped from dry twig to dry twig. They seemed to eat nothing but eggs, of which there was an abundant supply. The frog-birds were now all of medium or chicken size, and were always busy pulling small, thread-like worms out of the rotting wood, most of which was gone now; the frog-birds were clearly on their way out, but the rats were more plentiful, and getting bigger.

Soon the birds were gone, and only the now-big rats remained. They'd switched over to eating small invertebrates they dug out of the muddy soil under the mounds of rotted wood.

They began to run upright, holding their fore-limbs to their chests, like squirrels, only bigger, and without the fluffy tails.

"They're starting to look a lot like the Ylokk!" Helm exulted. "We must be close."

We were. In another few minutes we found ourselves crossing planes of reality where paved roads ran deviously across a peaceful, forested land, with villages in the distance. I slowed our rate of travel, and began fine-tuning the trans-net communicator; all I got was static until a loud, squeaky voice said, in Ylokk, or a close relative:

"Alert! Intruder on Phase One, second level! Slap squads move in!"

I was thinking that over when the shuttle slammed to a halt with a loud *bang*! The entropic flux gauge showed that we were in half-phase, neither in nor out of identity with the local A-line. We waited. After five minutes, Helm burst out: "What's happening? Where are we?"

"Nothing," I told him. "Nowhere. This is a null-temporal void between A-lines. They can't detect us here, because we're nowhere. Think of it as a plane of unrealized possibilities; not quite enough problyon flux-density to boost it through."

Somehow, that didn't seem to relieve him any. "What do we do now, sir?" he wanted to know. I wished I could tell him.

It seemed as good a time as any to eat and catch some sleep. I dozed off wondering just what the slap squad had in mind when they dumped us into null-time. Just the impulse to stop us, I decided. Helm was already snoring lightly. A fine and promising young officer, Anders Helm was, and it was entirely my responsibility to get him back home. I'd figure out how, later. Right now, I had to try to ease the traveler back into motion. According to some theorists, that was impossible. I guess I didn't entirely believe that, or I wouldn't have done what I had. On the other hand, maybe I was just a damned fool.

The best bet would be to rev up the field generator and build up the greatest flux-density possible, then slam into drive and hope to break through the entropic meniscus by brute force. But first—

This was an unparalleled opportunity to do a little EVA and make observations the technical boys back at HQ would cry hot tears of gratitude for. I thought about that, and then I thought about the fact that if things were such that I never came back, the young lieutenant would be doomed to a slow death, and nobody would do what had to be done about the Ylokk. Dumb idea. Right!

By that time I had buckled on my issue .38 and was cycling the hatch. As it opened, there was a slight *whoosh!* as air pressure equalized, in or out, I couldn't tell. Wan daylight showed me a landscape of undulating gray hills, with small and large pools reflecting the gray sky. Nothing moved in that landscape. The sky was a uniform lead-oxide color, with no cloud patterns showing. The air was cold, but fresh.

9

Somewhere a few light-years away, someone was yelling at me: "Colonel! Breathe! Please, take a deep breath!" I felt the pressure on my chest: the weight of a deep stratum of rock under which I lay buried. I relaxed a little, or tried to, and felt air *whoosh!* out of me. That reminded me of something. "Out," I decided. The outside air pressure was low. I had taken a lungful of near vacuum and fallen over. *Now Helm's got me back inside, and is trying to talk me into breathing in.* I thought about it. Hard work. *To Hell with it. Time to sleep.* I felt better, having let myself off the hook so nicely. Then the sediments built up another two hundred feet deep and I could feel my ribs creaking, getting ready to snap. That kind of worried me, so I took a deep breath and yelled, "All right! Lay off!" I started to sit up, but I'd forgotten those layers of limestone, basalt, and clay holding me down. Then there was an earthquake: the deep strata broke and thrust up and I felt my bones breaking now, but what did that matter? They were only petrified fossils buried in black muck. So I let that go, and wondered how a fellow could breathe under all that solid rock. Helm was bending over me, with his mouth hanging open, and it was his hard hands on my rib cage that were crushing me. I tried to take a swing at him, and found I had no arms, no legs, no body, just the awareness of pain and a desperate need to tell somebody.

"Easy," I heard somebody say. I wondered who it was, and gradually realized it was me. I got in a little more air and tried again:

"You're crushing my chest, Andy," I complained. I sounded like "Urriggaba . . ."

"Try to relax, sir." He withdrew a few inches. His face looked worried, poor lad. "I'm sorry, sir," he said, sounding like a fellow who was sorry. I wondered what about.

"It's been about a week since—after you . . ."

"Died," I supplied.

That remark made me suddenly aware of a thousand knives stabbing my chest, especially when I inhaled, which I did, just to check. That brought on a cough, which drove all the daggers an inch deeper.

"Sorry about that," I told him, or tried to. What I got was more coughing until I blanked out again. Then I was trying to curse and cough at the same time, which didn't work out well. I was furious with myself, first for being weak as American beer, and second for not being able to handle it. After a while I was sitting up and my arm was supporting me, with no aid from Helm.

Smovia's face hove into view. My ribs hurt, but

not as much, and the doc said, "There, you're feeling better now. I taped your ribs. Breathing better, too. I think you could take nourishment now."

"How about a small horse, shoes and all?" I suggested and didn't even cough.

"*Ja, då, för all del*," Helm spoke up, which the translator rendered as "Uh, well, OK." Not much in that, but then the lieutenant was never a very verbal sort of fellow. I knew he meant, "Gosh, sir, glad to see you're feeling better.

"I tried to stop the doc, here," he added in English, "but I guess he was right; you started breathing a lot easier once he taped you up. It looked too tight, but—"

"You did fine, Andy," I told him. "Just what the hell happened?" I was curious to know. "All I remember is opening up, and—zap."

"It's the air pressure, sir," he told me. "Seems on the phase of the Cosmic All, ah, in this A-line sir . . ."

"Go on," I prompted.

"Lots of argon, Colonel," he blurted. "We're way off-course, I'm afraid. C.H. date over four billion years. Atmosphere still forming. The planet ran into a gas-cloud, it appears, mostly argon. Breathable, but low pressure. It damn near collapsed your lungs, sir. Lots of blood there, for a while, and the doc here was carping about how foolish you'd been, but . . ."

Smovia was back. There was some more painful prodding and poking and I took a few deep breaths for the nice doctor-man, and started thinking about how much time was passing while I lay around repenting at leisure. I was draped in my command chair. On the screens I could see an expanse of mud flat.

"Helm," I called, weakly. He was right behind me. He came around, still looking anxious.

"How long did you say I was out?" I asked him. I tried to sit up and fell back with a *flump!* that made my head ring, even though it had impacted on a cushion.

"One week, sir," he told me grimly.

"Is the shuttle OK?" I asked Helm.

He nodded, still looking grim. "Mired in mud, but undamaged, as far as I could determine."

"Things here seem too normal," I remarked. In an entropic vacuole they were supposed to be different.

Helm edged close to me, arranging various expressions on his face. "There's one thing, Colonel," he told me like a fellow who hated to be the bearer of bad tidings. I waited for the punch line. It was a doozie.

"We've actually been here over a year," he said quietly, as if hoping not to overhear it. "The sun hasn't moved; it's the same day, but the chronometer in the shuttle is still running, and the calendar, too. One year, last week. This is the third time you've come to. You'll faint again in a few minutes."

"It hasn't been more than a couple of hours, subjective," I grumped. "The instruments must be wrong. We can't afford to be that long!"

"I know, sir," the lieutenant agreed mournfully.

This time I got an elbow under me. I waited while the little bright lights gradually faded, then got my feet onto the floor. "Where'd Swft go?" I asked. Helm just looked confused, like I felt.

"I need my boots," I said. Helm helped get

them on my feet, which I then planted on the floor. I was sitting on the edge of the command chair now, and I leaned forward until my weight was taken by my feet, and stood up. I didn't try to push with my legs, just imagined a skyhook lifting my butt, and then I was standing up. I felt a little dizzy for a moment, but that was just the sudden change in the altitude of my brain. The "oh boy, I'm going to faint" feeling passed and I tried a step; it worked OK. Helm was staring me in the face. "For a second, sir, your face looked greenish. It's all right now. But you'd better sit down and not overdo it this time."

I agreed wholeheartedly and sat on the edge of the chair.

"Nourishment," I said. "Rare roast beef and plenty of it, mashed potatoes and gravy, a slab of berry pie. A tall, cold, *Tre Kronor* beer."

"Sir, we have the issue rations," Helm reminded me.

"Recon Eggs Retief," I specified. "If we've been here a year," I said, doubting it, "why haven't we starved?"

"I don't know, sir," Helm admitted. "In fact, I don't really know much more than you do, sir, and *you've* been in a coma most of the time." He looked apologetic—apparently because he had suggested that maybe I didn't know everything.

"Maybe," he offered timidly, "we don't need nourishment in a null-time vacuole, or whatever you called it. Maybe our metabolism stops."

I shook my head. "If that were the case, we wouldn't be moving, and breathing, and discussing the matter. Let's just settle for not understanding it, like most people don't understand the Net, or like nobody understood the sun and moon until very recently. As a species, we got by in ignorance for the greater part of a million years. We used fire, even though we didn't know about 'oxidation.' " I realized I was trying to convince myself, and not succeeding. I thought about telling Helm to "carry on" and get out of here. It was just a passing thought, not something I really considered. Then I had another thought:

"Where's Smovia?"

"Sleeping, sir," Helm reported. "He's been sleeping a lot. I think he took something. He offered me one, but . . ."

"But you're not ready to become a hophead just yet," I supplied. "Good man, Andy." Then I started to say something encouraging, but that felt too phoney. So instead I pointed out that we were stranded in a rather inhospitable section of the Cosmic All.

"Right, sir," Andy replied briskly. Being content to not understand was a more comfortable intellectual position than eternally wondering. "But we still have the shuttle, sir," the boy reminded me brightly, as if that solved all our problems. "Intact," he added.

"I hate to tell you, Andy," I said hating to tell him, "but there are circuits in this machine that are chronodegradable. Security measure, you know, to prevent accidental use of a shuttle that might be abandoned in a line without A-technology. Also, environmental considerations made it seem like a good idea when we were designing it."

"But, Colonel, I thought . . ." Helm realized there was nothing to say and trailed off.

I nodded. "I'll get off a VR to the Director of Technology as soon as possible," I remarked sarcastically.

He jumped on that fast: "Good idea, sir. That'll . . ." He faded off. The comforting structure of established procedures didn't last long.

"Meanwhile," I said, "we at least have shelter. Minimal luxury, but better than sleeping in the mud."

"*Ja, då, för all del,*" he agreed, and looked at me anxiously. "We can't breathe the air out there, sir," he told me, a fact I'd discovered the hard way. "But there's enough oxygen in it to sustain us, after the filters concentrate it for us. But that means we're stuck inside here."

"So it does, my boy," I agreed airily. "Was there someplace out there you wanted to go?" I indicated the view through the small window: a glistening, fog-shrouded expanse of mud, dotted with puddles.

"It's not that, sir," he explained. "I just thought—well, we need exercise, and maybe, just over the horizon . . ."

"The planetary crust has just about stabilized, I'd say," was my next contribution. "The era of intense meteorite bombardment and constant volcanic eruption has apparently passed. The continents are stabilizing, and the water is in the process of accumulating in the sea basins. There won't be any land life, maybe no life at all. Distilled water and chemicals leached from the higher ground by the water flowing downslope. Probably just a few large lakes, so far; the land is so flat, the runoff doesn't channel to form a river. Instead of land and sea, there's just an endless mud flat. No icecaps yet. Not much variety in this world, I'm afraid."

"And yet this is contemporary with the twentieth century?" Helm queried.

"It's what the Zero-zero line would be like if a whole series of unlikely events hadn't occurred," I told him, "to create precisely the conditions required for the development of life."

"But, sir, how did primitive life affect things like ice ages and volcanism and all?" was his next anxious question, as if convincing me there *was* no such place would get us out of it.

"Consider," I suggested. "After the distilled-water seas were polluted by minerals from the land, plant life appeared. The first plant life, the algae, broke down the abundant carbon dioxide to release O-two into the atmosphere: the second great pollution, of the air this time, that made animal life possible. Animals like coral, for example, made reefs that affect oceanic currents. Then the accumulative plant debris gave rise to the coal beds, and of course the animals' exhalation of carbon dioxide, along with that produced by decaying plants, provided the greenhouse effect, which had a profound effect on climate, rainfall, erosion, and so on." I realized I was sounding like a high school science teacher holding forth, so I shut up. Helm didn't pursue the point, which was OK with me, because I was about out of glib explanations, anyway.

10

I had shown Helm how to operate the scanner, which I asked him to do. I went to the main panel to twiddle things there.

"The blue meter," he called. "It jumped!" I reassured him that was to be expected: it measured the entropic displacement between the shuttle and the external environment. Other readings were equally routine, until I came to the big one: temporal gradient. It read too high.

"There's over a thousand-year discontinuity," I stated.

"How?" he demanded. "If you mean——"

"I do," I confirmed. "We're marooned on a level where Charlemagne died just recently, back on the Zero-zero line."

"A rescue mission will never find us here," Helm said. He was peering out the open hatch at the shifting mists. "But neither will *they*," he added, more cheerfully.

I was staring, too. As a wisp of fog shifted I saw a shape, something that didn't belong in that landscape: a boxy, ornately decorated coach that needed only four handsome black geldings hitched to it to make an appropriate equipage for a queen. One door stood open, affording a glimpse of a purple satin interior.

"Stand fast," I told Helm. "I'm going to maneuver over next to it." I got into the pilot's seat, started up the terrain drive. Our shuttle had airtraction—it moved easily in spite of the mud, and I backed and filled until I could pull us alongside the carriage and match openings with it. Helm called, "Another inch, sir. There, that's perfect." I glanced up and saw a wavering pink aureole along the hatch where the two vehicles were in contact.

I went back, and he was looking curiously into the interior of the luxurious though primitive vehicle. There was a white-wrapped bundle on the seat. A wail came from it.

"*Djäveln!*" Helm blurted. "A baby!"

I stepped across into the coach, the physical contact with our shuttle creating an entropic seal that held back the external environment. The pink halo rippled, but held. It was temporal energy leakage from the imperfect temporal seal. I picked up the soft, blanket-wrapped bundle and looked at the face of a baby Ylokk. It was short-snouted, toothless and big-eyed. The grayish-tan pelt on the forehead was downy, and one small, chubby hand groped aimlessly. I was hooked. Helm was right behind me, and stumbled back when I stepped backward.

"Sir!" he exclaimed. "This odd conveyance. It's like the State Coach—it's more than it seems!"

I had already noticed the unobtrusive folding panel in the seat-back. Helm reached past me and opened it, revealing a fully-instrumented field-model console that could be nothing but a shuttle panel.

"The rats!" Helm blurted, at the sight of my bundle. "Why in the world did they abandon a baby here?" He was fingering the brocaded armorial bearings worked on the corner of the white blanket. "Obviously the child of a person of consequence," he said almost formally. As a loyal subject of the Swedish monarchy, he was very respectful of rank—even infant rank. I was moved more by the pup-appeal of a baby mammal, the same impulse that makes female dogs adopt newborn kittens, and a lady cat suckle baby rats. Anyway, we both knew we had to do something.

"If we leave him here, he'll just die," Helm said solemnly.

"No question about it," I agreed. "But we're not really set up to care for infants. No formula, no diapers, and especially no know-how."

"We'll have to take him home!" the lieutenant blurted. I handed him the kid.

"Swell," I agreed. "Where's home, and how do we get there?"

He looked hard at the small control panel. "Colonel," he started confidently, but continued in a more subdued tone, "can't we—can't *you*, sir, dope out the instruments and figure out how to return this thing to its point of origin? There must be a way . . ."

"Let's find it," I suggested. He began opening drawers and lifting things to look under them. Over the simple panel, which lacked most of the instruments essential to navigation in the Net, I spotted a small screen that looked right somehow. An adjacent manual trigger with a curious symbol caught my eye. I tripped it, and the screen went red, then pink, and finally resolved into a spider-web pattern that had to be pay dirt. Helm said so, sounding as if he'd just found his fondest wish under the *Jul* tree. "It's a map!" he told me happily. I was less pleased: I realized it was mainly a chart of Zone Yellow, with the rest of the Net only vaguely indicated.

"Easy," I cautioned him. "We don't know the scale. But that big nexus to the right of center is likely the Ylokk home base." I studied the pattern of faint intersecting lines, trying to match it up with my knowledge of the familiar Net charts of the Imperium, and the position of the black dot in the Zone on Manfred's big map. There was a tangled area off to the left lower corner, cut off by the edge of the screen. The lines there were snarled, many ending abruptly, some turning back on themselves.

"That's the most detailed map of the Blight I ever saw," I told Helm, pointing to the chaotic patch. "These fellows aren't *entirely* backward in their Net technology. That alone is worth the trip."

"But, sir, the Prince!" Andy blurted. "We *have* to return him home!"

"The Net specialists back in Stockholm Zero-zero will have a better chance of determining this buggy's PO than we do," I pointed out.

"Sir!" Helm blurted. "The, ah, carriage. We couldn't have come to this precise line by pure accident! They must have *wanted* us to find it!"

"Or somebody did," I amended. "Presumably someone concerned about the welfare of the baby."

"It hadn't been there long," Helm realized aloud. "It had a clean diaper."

"True," I concurred. "It seems we and this infant arrived at the same locus almost simultaneously. You're right: that's not likely to be purely a coincidence."

"Who?" Helm pondered. "Who'd want to maroon a baby—a *royal* baby—in a place like this? And why do it in a way that ensured the poor tyke'd be rescued?"

"Rescued?" I queried, without thinking. "He's still stuck here, just like us."

"But surely, sir . . ." Helm stammered, then straightened his back with a visible resolve. "But *you* know how, sir—we have the machine—and even the old coach—you said it's a shuttle, too!" He was warming to the idea. "We can use *it*. If necessary," he added.

"I don't know, Andy," I told him candidly. "We're in stasis here. We seem to experience subjective time, because that's how our nervous systems are wired. But how much time? The chronometer back in the shuttle said a year. What's a year? A concept of the human imagination—"

"Sir!" Helm broke in. "It's the time required for a single revolution of the earth around the sun! We didn't imagine *that*!"

"Sure we did," I corrected him. "It's still just an idea; maybe the idea fits a natural phenomenon pretty closely, or maybe that's another fantasy. The question hasn't yet been resolved by the philosophers."

"But sir—everybody knows—"

"For ages everybody knew the earth was flat," I reminded him, "and that the sun revolved around *it*."

"But *they* were wrong!" Helm pointed out, as if he'd made a telling point.

"Wrong? Any damn fool can look out across the sea, or a prairie, and *see* it's flat. And you just watch: the sun travels across the sky every day, and it rises over the horizon in the east just when it has to if it keeps traveling back under the earth all night. You're denying the obvious!"

"I see your point, sir. But we have the instruments that don't have any subjective bias; they show what's *really* happening."

"Jack up the drive wheels on a ground-car, and race the engine," I suggested. "The speedo will say you're doing eighty or ninety."

"*Really*," he corrected, "it just says the wheel the sensor is attached to is spinning. But that's a real phenomenon. The meter isn't imagining it."

"Which shows us how much human interpretation, based on preconceptions, goes into our understanding of even the most basic observation, Andy."

"Well," the young fellow started, "it doesn't really matter . . ."

"That's right. What we have to do is decide on a course of action, and do it. Actually, *I* have to make the decision. I can't fob the responsibility off on a junior officer."

He was nodding in agreement. "I didn't mean, sir . . ." He trailed off.

I told him I knew, and maneuvered away from the coach. It was finished in shiny black lacquer and looked brand new. There were solid rubber tires on its high, spoked wheels.

"It's a fake," I told Helm. "It was apparently intended to give us the idea we were looking for an A-line with a backward transportation technology. But that's synthetic lacquer and rubber. Let's find out what they were trying to conceal." I maneuvered back to match openings again, tighter, this time. The pink aureole sprang up. I stepped back inside, ducking my head under the low brocaded ceiling.

"Sir," Helm spoke up. "This could date from the nineties, when those two Italian fellows built the first, ah, shuttle. Maybe they wanted to disguise the machine—"

"Sure," I agreed. "Maybe. If so, this is a museum piece we have to take back home. In the meantime, I'm going to check it out." I got back out and climbed up to the elevated driver's seat. With no horses, the thing had to have a drive mechanism. It did. I called Helm up and showed him the controls concealed under the curved dashboard, which really was a functional barrier to the dirt thrown up by horses' hooves. I traced the connections and found a compact energy cell and a power lead to the left hind wheel. I touched the "go" lever and the high vehicle rolled smoothly forward a few inches.

"I was thinking, sir," Helm contributed as soon as he had climbed up beside me, still holding the sleeping infant. "Maybe whoever owns this buggy was running a few minutes behind schedule. They intended to phase in before we found the pup, and missed their coordinates just enough to let us get here before them."

"That's a possibility," I acknowledged. "But why would they leave the baby here, then decoy us here to find it, then come dashing to the rescue before we had time to react to the setup?" I wasn't expecting an answer, but went on silently pondering the question. Somebody, the Ylokk security boys, or another player not yet on the board, had gone to a great deal of trouble to waylay us. There was a reason for it, no doubt.

I told Helm to sit tight and be ready to drive, and went back down and got back in the shuttle.

I kind of hated to abandon the gleaming black coach in null-time; any museum in the Imperium would swap its collection of Jurassic dinosaurs for it. But I recorded the locus and told Helm to come down and strap in. Smovia had slept through finding the baby. I let him sleep. Poor fellow; he'd been on his feet ever since I'd brought Swft to him, at least twenty-four hours subjective, and I was planning to double-cross him.

"Andy," I addressed the lad gently, "I can try something, but I don't know what the result will be. This is a desperate expedient that's never been used in the field. It will either start us moving normally again, or eject us violently onto another entropic level. How do you vote?"

" 'Vote,' sir?" He sounded shocked. "It is my duty, sir, to follow the colonel's orders, sir . . ."

"All right," I agreed. I didn't want to upset him. "We'll do it. Try to relax and get some sleep."

I went forward to the console and pulled out the component trays, disconnecting the safety locks to do so. The theory was straightforward enough: even in an entropic vacuole, energies are flowing. Not the normal entropic and temporal energies of the problyon flux, but more esoteric if equally potent forces little noticed in a normal continuum. The insidious ninth force, for example, which causes the laws of "chance" to operate; and the tenth, which is responsible for the conservation of angular momentum, and which causes dust-grain-sized comets a light-year from the sun to execute a smart elliptical U-turn and head back Solward from out where Sol is simply the brightest star in sight. If I cross-controlled, applying control pressure tending to shift the shuttle from its present A-line, and at the same time cranked in entropic pressure tending to reverse our A-entropic motion, the two forces would be placed in direction opposition: the irresistible force would meet the irresistible force, and the shuttle would be squeezed like a watermelon seed until it popped out—or blew up.

I felt a little shaky. In the Net labs, we'd once tried a small-scale experiment involving only a single neutron, and it had blown the entire wing off into the realms of unrealized potential. But I didn't have any other ideas. It was only a moment's work to reverse the wave-guides and connectors to set it up: then I had to throw the DRIVE—FULL GAIN lever to see what would happen. The simple gray plastic knob looked pinkish— an entropic aureole indicating the leakage from the leashed energies of the universe. I threw the lever. The world blew up.

11

"—or at least that's what I thought," I was explaining to Andy, who was bending over me again.

"It seems like I'm always coming to with you giving me a worried look," I said.

He grinned and nodded. "There was quite a . . . well, a *wrench*ing, sir," he told me, as if that meant something. He looked around the cramped compartment as if he expected it—whatever "it" was—to happen again. "I felt . . . twisted, sir," he explained earnestly. "It lasted for maybe a second, but it seemed like a long time." He put a hand against his upper abdomen. "It felt *awful*, sir, but it passed, and everything was just like before, except that you were unconscious, sir. I just started to try to bring you around, and you started talking. Said it blew up, but it *didn't*, Colonel!" For once he didn't apologize for contradicting me.

"How's the view outside?" I wondered, and got

up easily enough and took the two steps necessary to look out the view-panel. I saw at once that the mudscape was gone. In its place was a bleak New Englandish day with leafless trees and wet leaves on the ground. A brisk wind seemed to be blowing, judging from the movement of the bare branches and the flying bits of vegetable matter. A spatter of rain was blowing with them. There was a cottage in sight, a hundred yards along a well-worn trail. It was half sod hut, half dugout. Light glowed from a window made of leaded bottle-bottoms. Smoke was rising from a crooked chimney that emerged from the sodden ground beside the biggest tree in sight. It gave an impression of an extensive underground installation, but it looked a lot cozier than the rest of the scene. While we watched, a tall Ylokk dressed in a red body-stocking came running on all fours from behind the house, if house it was, and along the trail, right up to the shuttle. The alien halted a few feet away, put nose to the ground, and went sniffing around our vehicle.

"Colonel," Helm spoke up. "He knows there's something here! Maybe——"

"Let's talk to him," I said and reached to switch on the outside talker, but I felt unsure of my command of the Ylokk speech. Swft had given me some pointers on the grammar—it wasn't too difficult—and between him and some cooperative prisoners we'd come up with a crash course in the basics, enough for a quickie hypno-tape. My time in the coder had been very short, though, with no time for the usual posthypnotics. I asked Helm if he knew the language. He didn't.

Then Smovia came groping out of his cubicle, rubbing his head.

"I had the damnedest dream," he muttered. "I

was caught in a typhoon and turned inside out. It was as real as *this* is—realer! Believe me, I was relieved to wake up and find my duodenum back where it belonged. What's going on—and what's *that*?" He was staring at the infant Helm was still holding. Helm showed him the baby-rat face, now in the repose of sleep.

"We . . . we found it," he explained. "It was—*he* was left in a fancy coach, sitting there in the mud. Poor little tyke."

"What coach?" Smovia demanded. "What mud?" He glanced outside and saw no answers out there.

"What's a baby doing *here*?" he wanted to know. "How did it *get* here? And where's 'here'?"

"I don't know," I told him. "The pup was in a disguised shuttle, like this one—but not one of ours—and I don't know, except that we're well into Zone Yellow. We've moved from there: it's a little more 'normal' here." I indicated the view of the road and the cottage.

" 'Zone Yellow'?" the doctor queried, at the same time taking the swaddled infant from Helm. "I seem to recall that. Didn't you say it's an inter- dicted area—not to be entered under any circum- stances?" He sounded more exasperated than scared.

"Normally, yes. But the trails the Ylokk left lead directly into the Zone; so it was decided that we had to make an exception."

"Why was it interdicted in the first place?" Doc asked me.

"We lost a shuttle, then others. After the third— the second two crews having been specially equipped and briefed—the decision was made to bypass the Zone in our exploration, and get back to it later, when presumably, we'd have improved our technology and could deal with whatever was swallowing our machines and crews."

"If *they* couldn't get back," Smovia demanded, "what makes you think *we* can?"

"I don't," I told him. "Not necessarily, at least. But I'm hoping—expecting—to learn something that will do the trick."

"Here—in this deserted village or whatever it is?" Smovia yelped, then diverted his attention to soothing the pup, which had awakened with a wail.

"My theory," I told him, "is that the Zone is another Blight, brought about, like our own, by Net experimentation gone wrong, but perhaps less severe. There's at least one island of relative normalcy here—the one our invaders came from. There may be others. I think we're close. I haven't done a complete analysis of the data our instruments have been storing, to find out if I'm right."

"Then let's do so—by all means," Smovia urged. "At once, Colonel, if you don't mind. Frankly, not knowing whether or not I'm to be added to the list of those lost in nowhere unsettles my digestion— not that I've had anything to digest lately. Shh, baby." He switched his attention back to the tot in his arms. "It's all right . . ." He paused and looked at me hopefully. "It *is* all right, isn't it, Colonel Bayard?"

"Look!" Helm broke in. He was pointing at the view panel, where a small group of tall, lean, forward-leaning creatures had appeared. Their tracks in the mud led back to a meandering line that disappeared in the distance.

"It's the rats!" Smovia gasped. "Probably looking for the baby! We'd better—"

Before he could finish that, one of the rats in

the van of the group glanced our way, saw something that interested him, and alerted the others. They crowded together and started our way in a menacing fashion. Then one groped in his overcoat pocket and brought out a .38 Smith & Wesson revolver—the issue weapon of the NSS. Clearly he was a veteran of the invasion, and this was his loot. He aimed it at the Ylokk in red, who was standing with his back to them, until the weapon bucked in the vet's long, narrow hand and the red one spun and fell on his back. The others at once scattered, ducking away in all directions and to the edge of our field of view.

"Colonel!" Helm blurted. "They murdered that fellow in cold blood!"

"I don't know the temperature of his vascular fluids," I countered, "but they shot him, all right."

Smovia had crowded in to look over my shoulder. "We must help that—uh—fellow," he decided. "The bullet struck him in the upper arm, I think. Probably he's not fatally wounded."

"Too bad, Doc," Helm supplied. "We can't. He's out there and we're in here."

The group of Ylokk were back; ignored the wounded one; they were snooping around the shuttle, as if they sensed its invisible presence.

"Those fellows know we're here," Helm volunteered. "The rats!"

"But," Smovia put in, "are they the kidnappers or did they come as rescuers?"

"They're the kidnappers," Helm stated. "You saw how they killed that fellow. They're obviously criminals."

"What if the one they shot was one of the kidnappers?" Smovia protested.

"Either way," Helm replied, "we can't just sit

here and let him bleed to death." He turned to me. "Colonel," he said heavily, "couldn't we get closer and use a hook to pull him in? That way—"

"You might be snatched into identity with the line," I pointed out. "It depends on the entropic gradient, which is reading off the scale, you recall."

The gang of Ylokk outside had moved entirely out of the wide-angle viewer's field of vision.

"The boy is right," Smovia said. "We must try. Have we a hook of some sort?"

"Standard equipment," I told him. "A telescoping one, stored in the locker there." The doctor got it out and was trying to maneuver it into a position in which it could be extended when Helm uttered a yell. I looked his way; the wounded Ylokk was crawling toward us. He got close and collapsed, one claw-like hand extended. I had to make a decision; that hand outstretched as if in appeal did it. I set up a closed-entropic field around the hatch and cycled it open. The wounded Ylokk groped as if puzzled, then a pointed snout appeared in the opening and I was looking at Swft, the general I'd last seen in the hospital. He recognized me a moment before I realized who he was.

"Colonel!" he gasped; he crawled inside another six inches and collapsed. Smovia had retreated with the baby, instinctively protective.

"We must . . ." Swft managed to gasp, and fell silent. Smovia came back, went to him, rolled him on his side, cut away his body-stocking, and began probing. He used an ugly-looking instrument and a moment later dropped a misshapen lump on a metal plate with a clatter that seemed too loud.

"Why the red longjohns?" I asked Swft.

"Caught unaware," he gasped. "No time to don my uniform."

"Clean wound," Smovia commented. "No bones or major vessels involved. Nerves are all right, too, I should imagine. I don't really know the anatomy very well, of course."

Swft uttered a high-pitched moan and rolled on his side. Smovia muttered and rolled him back, asked Helm to hold him there, and began applying medication. "Have to hold off infection, and kill the pain as well," he explained. He taped bandages in place and stood.

"Good as new in a few days," he predicted.

"But what are we going to do with a wounded rat for a few days?" Helm almost wailed. "Helping him, fine; but it's already crowded in here!"

"Easy," I said. "Throw him back out in the rain."

Helm and Smovia both stared at me; Smovia was grinning slightly.

"Sir! You wouldn't!" Helm blurted.

"That's right, I wouldn't," I told him. "You were about to suggest . . . ?"

"Well, Colonel," he offered, "as to that, I—" He let it hang, then, "Well, sir, I guess . . . I guess I was out of line—again."

"It's all right, Andy," I said. "That's how we all learn. Let's get him into a bunk."

"What bunk, sir?" Helm wanted to know.

"Yours," Smovia said. "You're junior officer here. They made me a lieutenant colonel."

"Later," I suggested, "we can clean out the auxiliary stores bin and fix him up in there."

"Sure, sir," Helm offered. "I'd be glad to—"

"The colonel said 'later,' son," Smovia reminded him.

Swft was stirring; his eyes opened and sought me. When we'd made eye contact, he gasped out,

"Colonel! We've got to get away from here at once! We're in the Desolation! You have no idea—!"

"I think maybe I do," I corrected him. "We have our own Blight, remember, surrounding the Zero-zero line."

He went on to describe the utter, well, desolation of the Desolation. Here, the gone-wrong experimentation had actually created a flaw, or discontinuity in the fundamental creation/destruction cycle, with the result we could see outside. Life hadn't prospered here.

"Who were the fellows who shot you?" I asked him out of context. He looked surprised, if I can read alien emotions.

"Why do you say I was shot?" he demanded.

"The doctor has just removed the slug," I told him.

" 'Slug'?" he queried. "Oh, one of your projective weapons. As you know, we have no such guns. So it was some of your chaps who, ah, shot me, eh?"

"It was a group of Ylokk," I corrected. "They seemed very interested in the coach."

This time, I *know* he was surprised. "Please explain," he begged. "Insofar as my briefing has informed me, a 'coach' is an animal-drawn conveyance no longer in common use."

"Except," Lieutenant Helm contributed, "for special circumstances, such as royal state ceremonies."

"Describe it," Swft came back tensely.

Helm did so.

"The armorial bearings," Swft persisted. "What—?"

"Sable, a griffon or," Helm told him. "On a bend argent, three mullets of the first."

Swft nodded, then with a sudden *snap!* of his needle-sharp teeth, twitched and rolled to all fours.

"I see it, now," he hissed. "A vile plot within a plot, hatched within the palace itself—" He broke off and twisted his head to stare up at me. "But what have *you*—?"

"Nothing," I informed him. "We came along and stumbled on the coach, just sitting there—"

"The draft animals, the kwines," he demanded. "The attendants—?"

"No coachman," I told him. "No footmen. No nursemaid—"

He broke in with a yell. "What of the prince?"

"There *was* no prince," Smovia spoke up. I looked at him, feeling surprised. Why was he lying?

He glanced my way. "More of a princess," he told me in Swedish, which it seemed hadn't been included in Swft's briefing. The general had retreated as far as he could into the corner, and was still baring those big incisors of his.

"Easy, General," I started, but Swft burst out, "Then how . . . ?" He lowered his voice. "Why did you say there should be a nursemaid? Eh? Speak up! I warn you, I'm not to be trifled with in this matter! Speak!"

"Mind your tone!" Helm interjected. "You will address the colonel with respect, sir!"

"Of course," Swft muttered. He was visibly pulling himself together. "I beg of you, Colonel Bayard, if you know of anything of—" He changed his tack. "The swine who shot me. Where did they go?"

"They ran off," I told him. "We couldn't see where."

"I saw them," Swft said coldly. "But I hardly imagined such personages would stoop to attempted murder. There was the Lord Privy Seal, Sctl, and General Rstl, and some young fellows of the Guard, and—treachery!" he wailed. "Treachery on a grand scale! It is not to be borne!"

"Relax, for now, Swft," I suggested; then, to Smovia, "show him the baby." He nodded and ducked into his cubicle and a moment later handed the sleeping infant to the wounded general, now on his hind feet and making small, ecstatic noises.

"Your Royal Highness," he crooned, looking down at the small face. He looked up at me. "He's all right? They didn't?" Just then the baby uttered a squall and Swft almost dropped her.

"Why is it, General," I asked him, "that you refer to this little female as 'him'?"

" 'Female'?" He almost dropped her again. Smovia stepped in and reclaimed the tot.

"Can it be?" Swft inquired of himself. "Is it possible that we all—that the entire Movement is based on a lie? But of course! That explains a great deal!"

"I guess I'm slow," I said. "I still don't get it."

"Gentlemen," he addressed us formally, "the Noblest of All is in your debt. The Governance itself must acknowledge that debt. I thank you."

"You think these fellows would have harmed the baby?" I wanted to know.

"They would have killed him—or especially *her*," he answered me. "You see, great issues devolve on the matter of succession. This child, who certain traitors claim is an impostor, is the key to the fate of Great Ylokk. We must conduct ourselves with great circumspection, lest we precipitate yet another disaster to add to those which have already befallen Great Ylokk."

"Like your damn-fool invasion," I suggested. To my surprise, he nodded. "I did what I could," he said.

"Wait a moment," I cut in. "You told me all about how it was *your* idea."

He looked at his feet. "Either way my honor is compromised," he muttered. "I lied to you, Colonel; I was under sentence of death for my opposition to a scheme already endorsed by the Noblest. It was Grgsdn who— Never mind. I was unable, Colonel, to admit that I had been dominated by another, coerced. I had to pretend, even to myself, to be in control of matters. You should have let me die."

"It's not quite that bad to be shown up as a fool," I comforted him. "It's happened to me plenty of times. You'll survive. Who's this 'Grgsdn' character?"

Swft showed his incisors in a snarl. "He is an elusive scoundrel and rabble-rousing treacher whose vile counsels have been insinuated into the deliberations of the governance. He hopes to overthrow the ancient dynasty and place his own unspeakable clan in the Jade Palace!" The general broke off, apparently overcome by the enormity of whatever he was talking about.

"What does the baby have to do with all this?" I pressed him. "And why abandon her here in Zone Yellow?"

Swft shuddered. "They would have challenged the Noblest," he snarled. "Defied her to show the presumed heir. When she was unable to do so, the entire structure would have come crashing down. The little of peace and order that has survived the Killing would have dissolved in chaos. I had hoped, perhaps"—he paused and gave me a sideways look with those disconcerting red eyes— "somehow, this adventure—the invasion—might disrupt their plan, and allow me the opportunity to rally the forces of Right. Otherwise . . ."

"Oh, 'the forces of Right,' eh?" I queried. "That means 'our side,' I believe. Which side *that* is depends on who's talking."

"My cause *is* Right!" Swft insisted. "Consider: the Royal House has governed wisely for ten millennia, since the Conqueror imposed peace among the barons. Until the Killing came, that is. The plague has thrown our world into chaos. There are always dissenters, of course. Was not Evon cast out of Paradise? They seized upon the disorder to gain a following, blaming the Killing on the Great House. A false puppet claimant to the throne rose up, and hordes of the ignorant hailed her, hoping for favor after the installation of this upstart in the Jade Palace. Grgsdn himself is seldom seen, which merely adds to his allure. His disciples spread his foolish message. Fools! This would have exchanged the ancient order for a new regime of venality and expediency, hoping for personal advantage!"

12

"That's very unfortunate, General," I told him carefully, aware that the conversation was being recorded. "But it is the policy of the Imperium to avoid any interference in the internal affairs of other A-lines."

"But it is more than a mere internal squabble, Colonel," Swft protested. "Before the advent of these 'Two-Law' scoundrels as they call themselves, Ylokk was a peaceful land, rich in all that made life livable. Our forests yielded a wealth of nuts and fruits, as well as our staple tubers and fungi. We lived well, noble and simple alike, with plenty for all, free for the gathering. Then the TL people began to agitate, telling folk that they should be called upon to make no effort in order to obtain food and shelter—that the Royal House should provide everything, neatly packaged.

"Our gathering festivals had been joyous occasions, when all, high and low, went into the virgin greenwood to select their year's subsistence. Those who were more diligent ate better. The TL troublemakers attacked this, saying that all should fare alike."

"What's this 'Two-Law' business?" Andy interrupted.

"These cretins," Swft said harshly, "have the curious notion that Natural Law is subject to manipulation, indeed to repeal. We all know of the three great laws of motion. The revolutionists claim, arbitrarily, that the law which states that 'for every action there is an equal and opposite reaction' is a contrivance of the Great House, and that indeed only two laws of motion are fundamental."

"Is that Newton's first or third law, sir?" Helm asked me.

I didn't know. "It's another way of saying 'you don't get something for nothing'," I told him. "And these con artists are actually able to convince people they can change that?" I asked Swft incredulously.

"All too easily," he said. "Since it is precisely what they want to hear. 'Why labor in the forest?' they now demand, 'When the royal yilp-proof silos could dispense largesse to all?' "

"Don't they wonder how those silos are going to be filled?" Andy asked.

"By no means; Grgsdn and his foolish followers tell them the Noble clan can be set to full-time gathering. Alas, even that unequitable expedient would avail nothing; there are too few nobles. Their ancestors, after all, were granted Noble rank on the basis of their prowess in food-gathering for the commonweal. Only a few have ever attained such rank, which is hereditary only in the lifetime of the first lord, so that one who has labored mightily may count among his rewards the security of seeing his grandchildren and even great-grands prosper in life. That old order of peace and prosperity has been thrown into disarray by these insidious propagandists. All organized effort has come to a halt; the people starve, unless they resort to cannibalism, which of course leads to epidemic, culminating in the Killing. Then Grgsdn's minions stormed the Skein Compound, discovered for themselves our capability for exploration of the cosmos of alternate energy-states, and declared their Crusade—"

"Meaning the invasion," Helm interpreted.

"Actually a slave-raid on a grand scale," Swft confessed. "Its purpose being to acquire cheap labor to replace the normal efforts of the Folk."

"Dumb idea," I commented.

"As I see now, all too well," Swft agreed, shaking his head. "I suppose I, too, was deluded to some extent by the concept of eternal leisure for all, while a subject species toiled for us. So you see," he concluded, "our internal strife has become a matter of common cause to both our species."

"What do you expect *us* to do about it?" I asked him. "I see now why you took the risk of coming out to find us. We're your only contact with humanity, and your only hope."

"You could quite easily overwhelm and disarm the TL jackals," Swft stated, as if it were actually too obvious to go into detail about. "Your clever weapons alone will persuade them to withdraw and cease their activities. We are, as I have said, not a warlike folk."

"Are these revolutionaries concentrated in one spot, where they can be rounded up and disarmed?" Helm queried. "I wouldn't mind helping in that job."

Swft wagged his head in his disconcerting way: he had gotten his signals crossed and nodded for negative and shook for confirmation. "They have seized the Jade Palace and the governmental complex," he told us. "And of course, the technical compound. All their leaders are there, but their deluded followers are everywhere."

"That's an odd name, 'Grgsdn'," I commented. "I've noticed most of your names are of one syllable."

"He's a strange fellow," Swft agreed. "Appeared out of nowhere and began agitation at once. Rumors of his curious activities are rife. I was remiss in not investigating him at once. Then the Two-Law ideology burst upon the good folk of Ylokk, with its attendant treacheries, and it was too late to lay him by the heels. His HQ is secret, and moves frequently."

"If we captured this Grgsdn," I suggested, "and he publicly recanted and told people to go back to their normal ways, would that put an end to the insurrection?"

"I've considered that possibility carefully," Swft said, "envisioning myself as his captor, of course; but the issue is doubtful, the TL dogma being so appealing to so many. But now," he went on, "with the princess safely in our custody, we can give the lie to their vile claim that the Noble House is in decline, unable to produce an heir to be the next empress. I'm sure that the great mass of the decent folk yearn for a return to the old ways. Yes, now we can do it! Will you?" he appealed. From Smovia's cubicle the baby wailed.

"What do you say, Andy?" I consulted my young aide. "Shall we give it a try?"

"I'm for it, sir!" he came back enthusiastically. "But of course, sir, I can hardly . . ."

"You can't say so, Lieutenant," I reminded him. Then, to Swft, "It's a deal, General. We help you and the invasion is off."

"By all means! Gladly. We will never forget your magnanimity!" he blurted.

"I can't guarantee anything," I reminded him. "What's the building you came out of?"

"Our field HQ," he told me. "An auxiliary installation few know of."

"And the fellows who shot you?"

He nodded in negation. "No one could have—"

"Somebody left the baby," I reminded him. "Maybe they were coming back after it. By the way, why were *you* there?"

"A routine inspection, nothing else." Swft brushed the question aside. "After all, my duties—"

"Were you chasing those fellows, General?" I asked. "Or were they chasing you?"

"Impossible," Swft gasped out. "Our most closely guarded secrets—"

"I guess the baby was closely guarded, too," I suggested. Swft tried to sit up, an awkward position at best for one of his snaky build.

"Colonel," he addressed me seriously. "The disaffection runs deeper than I had suspected, it appears. If Grgsdn's agents were able to penetrate the Jade Palace itself, then the complex, there is a traitor at work very close to the Empress. I don't know . . ." He passed out then, and Smovia hurried over to see to him.

13

"Colonel, sir," Helm addressed me earnestly. "Let's do it. Let's help him. If what he says is true—"

"That's the key point, Lieutenant," I cut in. "For all we know, Swft himself may be the kidnapper and the leader of the revolt, if there *is* a revolt."

"I doubt it, sir," Helm said, sounding dubious. "Those fellows *did* shoot him down on sight. I don't think honest folks would do that."

"They might if they're the Imperial Guard, after a princessnapper," I offered.

"He lied to you before," Helm reminded himself. "All about how the invasion was his idea and all."

"Sure, but I didn't believe that," I said. "The Supreme Commander wouldn't be hanging around on his own, outside the main battle area."

"We could go and take a look," Helm offered.

"He didn't even know his precious stolen baby was a female," I thought aloud. "Don't you think a loyal general officer of the Empress would know that?"

"Not if it was an official secret," Andy countered.

"Why would that be a state secret?" I demanded.

"Because," Swft spoke up from his position on the deck, "the birth of a legitimate heiress apparent would be a big boost to the Loyalist cause, and the baby would be an obvious target. So the Palace announced the birth of a son instead, to minimize the reaction."

"Useless; the word was bound to leak pretty soon," Andy hazarded. "They could pretty well dictate terms."

"Precisely," Swft agreed. "Indeed, if her existence was known, it would be seen as a threat by Grgsdn's faction. But the ruse at least ensured Her Highness's safety, insofar as the plotters are concerned."

"But why did you abandon her in the Zone?" I asked him.

He looked at me blankly. "Very well," he conceded. "I did spirit Her Highness away, to save her life. Somehow they followed me; I was forced to leave the coach in half-phase, and resort to the station, in order—" He interrupted himself. "I detected your presence here," he grumped. "This locus is a state secret." He gave me a "this is between us" look. "Experimental, you know."

I nodded as if I knew what that meant.

Swft looked out at the bleak landscape. "Temporarily they are thwarted," he continued, "but I see no basis for optimism inherent in our present situation. This is a very inhospitable phase," he went on. "It taxed our resources even to erect the modest installation you see there. There is no indigenous life, there's nothing to eat. All supplies must be transferred in, and all waste hauled out, in accordance with Governance policy."

"Ours, too," I told him. "What about the close adjacent lines?"

"No better," the alien general said. "We are, after all, in the Desolation."

"We call it Zone Yellow," I said, "and our tentative explorations here were no more encouraging."

"Our location is compromised. They will strike again," Swft stated, with a faint revival of enthusiasm. "We must depart here as soon as possible." He paused to look dubious. I was getting better at reading his limited expressions. "Right, Colonel?" he said like a fellow expecting prompt agreement.

"I don't know that that's possible. We had a breakdown of some sort. I hadn't planned on stopping here."

"You may blame or credit me with that, Colonel," he said. "It was I who erected the barrier field to halt you. I regret the necessity, but of course, it *was* necessary."

"How did you know we were coming this way?" was my next query.

He made a sort of shrugging motion, something else he'd picked up from the humongs; but his physique wasn't built for it. "We have rather sophisticated tracking devices," he stated. "I knew that someone, probably yourself, Colonel, would follow me home, so I focused a device on the first traveler to set out on my trail, and stopped you here, at my out-station."

"I guess it *was* pretty dumb to follow your tracks directly," I conceded.

He waved that away. "Hardly, sir. You had no choice. Here in the Desolation one may circle for eternity, without a path to follow." He did a passable shudder. "A fate too dismal to contemplate," he added.

"Our present situation doesn't seem much different," I commented, "except that we're stationary for eternity."

"By no means, Colonel," Swft objected. "You forget my station there." He waved toward the view-panel. "If you will maneuver your vehicle into position at the entropic lock, around to the side there . . ." I looked and saw what appeared to be a cellar door set at a slant against the wall.

"Simply tuck in there, and match entropic energies, and we'll be safely inside in a moment," Swft said confidently.

"Colonel!" Helm blurted. "If we didn't match frequencies perfectly when we tried to cross, wouldn't that blow us to—?" He trailed off as he realized he didn't know, and couldn't even imagine *where* it would blow us.

"It would, Andy," I continued. "*If* we didn't match frequencies, problyon flux, and a few other variables. I don't propose to be so careless." I didn't even consider refusing to try; the prospect of escape from this dead-end was attractive enough to overcome any amount of caution.

So for the second time, I ground-maneuvered the shuttle, something regulations say not to do except in case of "ultimate necessity"; I figured this qualified. This time I had a road to follow; Swft's out-station was apparently set up to receive lots of traffic. Up close the cottage appeared to be made of concrete, carefully textured and weathered to present the appearance of a primitive clapboard structure. The small door, seemingly of dead-nailed, rough-sawn planks, was set above grade; I had to levitate the shuttle a few inches on its air-cushion gear. Once in alignment, I locked in to the local gradient. Looking at Swft, I asked him:

"Any special maneuvers at this point?"

"Allow me, Colonel," he said, and went to the panel and made a couple of adjustments with practical ease. The pink aureole sprang up and faded to lavender, then a cold blue. Swft called, "Ready, sir. Permission to open up."

"It's your neck, too," I replied. "And Her Highness's."

"Wait a minute!" Smovia spoke up. He was holding the baby again. Someday the young fellow would make a good father. "Do you propose to risk harm to this infant, Colonel?"

"We're all in this together, Doctor," I reminded him. "It's the only way to get her—and us—out of limbo."

"Sorry, sir. Of course," he apologized. I gave Swft the nod.

The lights went out. Helm yelped, "Colonel! It's dark!"

"An acute observation, Lieutenant," I said, sounding a little more sarcastic than I had intended. "Relax," I added, trying to sound less harsh. After all, this was the boy's first trip out-line, and he hadn't had the normal six-weeks' indoctrination.

"It's just a momentary stasis, while our entropic potential matches up that last fraction of a problyon," I explained, feeling a need to explain the explanation.

Swft adjusted controls and the light returned. He asked permission to debark; I nodded and he stepped through. I followed, experiencing no unusual sensation as I crossed over. Helm came behind me. We were in a neglected-looking storeroom, with shelving sagging under a few hefty cartons and some plastic-wrapped electronic subassemblies, all under a layer of gray dust.

Swft led the way through a door, this one a seamless composite panel, into a laboratory-like space with lots of unfamiliar apparatus and a few recognizable items, very high-tech. There was less dust here, and better light. Swft went directly to a section of workbench with a well-used look, flipped a switch, and began studying instrument readings intently. He didn't sit down, just sort of curled over the bench. It looked awkward to me, but then *I* wasn't six-four and twelve inches in diameter.

"Good," he said cheerfully, and uncoiled. We waited for more.

"Potential is at operational level, coherence is uncompromised," he stated comfortably. "I was a bit worried, actually, with those fellows interfering, laying noncomputed trails, but the basic field is undisturbed. Are you ready to depart at once, gentlemen?"

"First," I insisted, "tell us why and how you trapped us in the precise locus where the coach was parked."

"As to that," he started, like a fellow getting ready to concoct a lie, "that was almost accidental. Of course, your vector-extrapolation indicated you'd pass that way and likely detect the vehicle's field. I acted in haste, thinking only of protecting Her Highness."

"I see," I told him, and I did, sort of. "And why did you come running out of your office in your underwear?"

"I was monitoring the screens, of course, and

when you phased in, I was unsure if it was indeed you, or the enemies of the Jade Palace. I knew the position of your shuttle—the coordinates were displayed along with the alarm signal—but when I stepped outside, I saw nothing. I hurried to the spot where you *should* have been, and in fact, were, of course—in half-phase, with the result you witnessed."

"Sure," I conceded. "Careless of you, if you expected your enemies. But how do we know they're not the good guys, and you're not the villain?"

"I can only pledge my word, on my honor as a peer of the Noble Folk," he said, not as if he expected me to be much impressed. But for some reason, I believed him; somehow, he'd managed to make a favorable impression on me, wounded and captured as he was. I gave him my hand on it. He took it awkwardly.

"What's the drill, General?" I wanted to know. "I take it you have a shuttle of some kind here?"

"None needed, Colonel," he corrected me. "I have a transfer chamber, which will shift our primary awareness, with precision, to whatever coordinates in the space/time/vug continuum we may select, though temporal maneuverability is minimal. This way, please."

14

It was an unexceptional-looking little booth, walled off in the center of a big, garage-like space, with banks of tightly-wound M-C coils or their equivalent packed up against the walls and across the ceiling. Inside, there were padded benches, the wrong size and shape for human anatomy. Swft made a few adjustments and converted a couple to flat, bunk-like affairs that would fit anybody.

"I must caution you, gentlemen," he announced, as soon as he'd gotten Smovia and the baby comfortably settled, while Helm and I shifted for ourselves, "that you will experience, shall I say, 'unusual' sensations during the transfer, which lasts for only a few milliseconds of subjective time. Feel free to cry out if you wish, but do *not* move." He stepped outside and closed the door on us.

I had a few hundred important questions I

needed to ask, but before I could decide to go after him, the unusual sensations started up. It was almost indescribable: it included an uneasy sensation up under the ribs, in the solar plexus area, and a hot-needles feeling on the backs of my hands and the top of my thighs. It wasn't painful, but was by far the most horrible sensation I ever experienced, worse than nausea and pain combined. I hung on and wished it would go away. I thought of looking at Smovia and Helm to see how they were taking it, but it was just a thought: the thought that I was in over my head and death was next. But after a while it faded out and left me feeling slightly confused but OK.

Smovia was already on his feet. Helm was slumped, out cold. Smovia slapped the backs of his hands and got him up, groggy but functioning. I said:

"What was that all about, doctor? What kind of sensation *was* that?"

"Something quite outside the realm of medical science as we understand it today," he told me.

Helm made a gargling sound and said, "And I died. I know I was dying. But you're still here, Doc, so I guess— Well, you could be dead, too. Where are we?"

"We're in a transfer booth in General Swft's out-station," I reminded him.

"Where is he?" Smovia demanded, not unreasonably.

"He just stepped out, right before the feeling," I informed him.

Helm lurched toward the door. I told him to hold on.

"Presumably," I said, "we've been transferred

to a receiving booth in the Ylokk capital. We'd better go slowly."

"Happened too fast," Helm supplied. "We came in here, and just as I got settled, zap! I was dying." He looked at me appealingly.

"I really was," he insisted. "I could feel myself *adrift*; I know it was a change-over to another level of being. Death."

"Not quite," I corrected. "It was another kind of change-over. We moved across the continua to another A-line. We're still alive, don't worry."

"*Ja då, för all del*," the lad agreed, nodding. "But we crossed plenty of alternate A-lines in the shuttle, and nobody died—or felt like it."

"We were protected by the circuitry of the shuttle," I explained to him and myself. "This time we were exposed to the subjectively accelerated entropic flow, unshielded, something we usually experience at a much slower rate. This movement is associated in our deep minds with death, hence the horrible sensation."

He looked around. "I notice Swft isn't here," he stated. "Damned rat probably abandoned us here to die."

"He just stepped out," I reassured him for some reason. Just then the enemy general stepped back in.

"Gentlemen," Swft said abruptly, "I have deposited us in an abandoned warehouse near the Complex. The streets are dark, and few passersby should be here. We must step out cautiously— after I have scanned our surroundings, of course." He slithered into one of the curiously-shaped chairs before a panel containing three ranks of small repeater screens, all of which were dark. He seemed to be satisfied, though, and got up and opened the exit door.

"Take care," Swft cautioned. "There may be a slight disorientation, due to a small error of closure in the entropic gradient. Allow me." He didn't wait for assent, but stepped out, and we followed him.

The bells were so close, they must be, I decided, inside my head. *Clong! Cuh-long! Ong-ong!* I grabbed my skull with both hands and tried to back away from the din, but it only got louder, closer, surrounding me, driving me to desperation. "Stop it!" I yelled, and willed the noise to stop.

"Stop!" a great voice boomed out. I got my eyes open against the weight of the clangor and saw Swft, sleek, handsome, a figure of dignity and nobility, to whom I was privileged to say, "The noise! It's driving me—" I couldn't say any more with the big spike driving into my chest. I saw that we were in a deserted street with pole lights and brick facades, and a vile odor of rotting flesh. Dead rats lay everywhere.

"Easy, Colonel," the General ordered me. I tried, and the pain, along with the noise, began to fade.

"It's your heart you're hearing," he was telling me. "Ordinarily, your auditory cortex suppresses awareness of it. Relax, now, and just let it fade away."

I saw Helm, slumped against a light-pole, gagging.

"It's going to be all right, Andy," I tried to say. Doc Smovia staggered into my field of vision, green-faced, hugging the baby, who was still sleeping peacefully. The noise was gone as if it had never been. My chest felt all right, too. I steadied Smovia and took the infant and passed her to the general. Andy was blinking at me. "Colonel!" he gasped out. "Where . . . where . . . did—?"

"It's all in our minds, Lieutenant," I reassured him. " 'Error of closure,' His Excellency called it."

Smovia seemed back to normal. He looked a little pale in the light of a sodium-vapor lamp, but then everybody looks dead in that light. It wasn't just him: the whole street had that same wan, dirty-yellow look, just like I felt. The scene was as horrible as the stench.

"You mentioned a warehouse, Excellency," I said, feeling not quite sure what that meant.

"Of course." He indicated an open door in a corrugated-metal wall beside us. "We have only just emerged," he explained. "You were a bit confused, but you followed me when I came out, the coast being clear. By the way," he went on, "I know the idiom 'the coast is clear,' but find it most obscure. What is its derivation?"

"Is that a big issue right now, sir?" I wondered aloud, fighting the paradigm. The general actually looked a little scruffy, I noticed. He was an ugly fellow, if you tried to see him as human, which he wasn't, so I tried to regain the rat's-eye view I'd had for a moment, and succeeded so well that I had to move over against the wall, for security, as a surge of agoraphobia hit me. Andy and Smovia were already there, huddled against the sheet-metal door. I wanted desperately to please the general.

The feeling faded, and he was just an overgrown rat in a dowdy raincoat, standing in a deserted street, sniffing the foul air and twitching his whiskers.

"This way," he squeaked. "Hurry!"—and started off without looking to see if anyone was following. We got ten feet before a whistle shrilled, and somebody yelled. Swft did a hard left turn into a narrow air space between age-blackened brick walls, and we followed. Our feet crunched on trash underfoot. After a few yards, the cramped alley opened into an eight-foot-square air shaft.

"Now what?" Andy expressed my thought precisely. Smovia stayed close to the wall and cautiously edged around to the far side, looking back down the alleyway.

"There are—people—there," Smovia managed to utter. "We're trapped!" he accused Swft, who stooped and lifted a square manhole cover.

"We must descend, quickly," he said urgently, and started down. Ten seconds later I assisted Smovia down the last few rungs, he being burdened once again with the baby. We were now trapped in a slightly larger space than the air shaft above. Swft replaced the cover and we were in total darkness. At least there was no stench here.

"We came here," I reminded the Ylokk, "to do a little job of world-saving. How do you intend to manage that from this coal cellar?"

"No, merely a utility space," he corrected me offhandedly. "Kindly observe—closely." He went to the nearest of the rough stonework walls, reached up as high as he could reach, and began to grope over the surface with his long-fingered hands. A stone nearby slid aside; at the same time a dim light sprang up, revealing a narrow crawl-space. He motioned me in impatiently.

I stood fast. "What's all this hocus-pocus?" I wanted to know first. "Why didn't you drop us right at our destination, whatever that is?"

" 'The Map Room,' we call it," he supplied. "Alas, our transfer method is not yet fully perfected. It lacks absolute precision with reference to the first three dimensions. Vug-wise, though, and temporally it's quite accurate." He broke off his speech and went headfirst into the hole without waiting for my response. I looked at Helm and Smovia. The doc gave a little shrug and started into the hole. I hauled him back, just as Helm burst out:

"Why should we trust that rat?"

"Because Doctor Smovia has the baby," I told him, and he ducked his head and went in. That was a little pushy of him, but I let him go. Smovia handed me the baby and without waiting for permission, followed Helm. This time, burdened with the infant, I got to the opening just as his feet disappeared inside. I groped, but he was gone and so was the opening. That left me and one peacefully sleeping rat-pup, alone in a cell.

Baby began fretting again. I patted her and tried to come up with a brilliant idea. The best I could do was reflect that Swft would hardly have abandoned his precious princess for good. That gave me another idea. I took her over and put her gently inside the hole that had swallowed up Andy and the doc. It wasn't wide enough for my shoulders. Smovia and Andy were slim fellows, so they'd gotten in easily. I knew I couldn't make it in there; no way out for me. But Swft would be back, and before I'd grown a full beard.

I stretched out on one of the S-shaped benches as well as I could and went to sleep before I had figured out just what to do with my feet.

15

When I woke, I was cold, stiff, and aching in most places. Sitting up was no fun. I was dizzy, and had a pain in my stomach.

I looked around the bare room; it didn't look any different. I went over and tried to remember just what Swft had done to open his secret passage to nowhere. I remembered he'd had a little trouble reaching the magic spot with his stubby arms. I scanned the joints in the stonework up just under the ceiling and thought I saw a slightly discolored spot. I felt over it, and the light, the source of which I couldn't make out, dimmed. I quit messing with the wall. Things were bad enough without being in the dark. I felt a little disappointed in myself. I'd really done a swell job: I'd handled things just right. I'd gotten myself separated from my troops and locked in a cell that could become dark at any moment. That reminded me of the shaft we'd entered by. I recalled that it was near the middle of the chamber, and looked up. Apparently my recollection was wrong, because there wasn't any panel there or elsewhere. Double swell.

Just then a door that hadn't been there a minute ago opened beside me and Swft walked in.

"Sorry to have been delayed," he remarked casually. He glanced at me inquiringly and asked, "Where are the other fellows—and Her Highness?" sounding more curious than worried.

"They went in the hole after you," I told him.

"Nonsense," he replied crisply. "It's only . . ." He waved a hand in the direction of the hole. "One could hardly, ah . . . As you saw, it's not large enough to hold two humongs, and besides that, it's empty."

"It held you all right," I pointed out.

He nodded agreement; at least he'd finally gotten that gesture sorted out. "But of course, I, that is, one *must* know—" He broke off. "Dear me," he continued. "I fear, my dear Colonel, that something really quite unfortunate has occurred."

"Tell me about it," I urged. He half sat, half coiled beside me.

"You see," he began.

"No, I don't." I cut him off.

"This is a very special entryway to the Map Room," he started again. "This room is, of course, protected by multiple entropic barriers. The entry here threads its way tortuously through a most complex suture, or pattern of sutures to be quite precise, and only those knowing the formula can negotiate it. Only one person besides myself knows the equations. Your associates, I fear, are now lost in an unreachable phase of space/time/vug. This is horrible."

"You can save the crocodile tears," I told him. "You seem to forget you invited me in there, and I don't recall you whispering any secrets to me."

"I would have, dear fellow," he assured me. "The first key is simply the familiar quadratic equation."

"I never did get it straight whether the 2A was under just the minus 4AC, or the square root of B squared, too."

"No need to fret," he told me. "We'll be using another route."

"What about Lieutenant Helm and Doctor Smovia?" I demanded.

"Perhaps," he mused, "if I direct the Master Computer to analyze the disturbance-pattern in the Grid at the moment of their entry . . ."

"Where's this Master Computer?" I asked him.

He said, "Follow me closely, Colonel, and I shall escort you there. It's not far." He went back out the door, which was still there, and I was right on his heels, wondering if I had missed something important. That didn't comfort me, but it did make me take careful note of the route we were following, along a smooth-paneled corridor with flush ceiling lights and a crack in the stone floor. To lay a trail, I started dropping bits of the requisition form I found in my pocket. Swft went silently along, not quite stealthily, but making no unnecessary sounds.

"Enemy territory?" I asked him. He made a curt *shush!*ing motion, and kept going. Finally, he stopped in wider space where a cross-corridor intersected. He hesitated a moment, then did a hard left. He'd gone about three of his silent steps when a rat bigger than him leapt from the passage to the right, missed its first pass at him with a curved dagger, and rounded on me. Swft heard a sound and turned quickly. By then, the big rat was on top of me, not using the knife, but snapping his incisors too close to my throat for comfort. I got my right arm clear and socked him hard in the short ribs; he folded over, then fell, threshing on the smooth tiled floor. I stepped on the hand that was holding the nasty-looking knife until I heard bones crack. Swft was beside me.

"Incredible! You've bested one of the Three Hundred, our elite guard force. That simply does *not* happen!" He was looking at me with what I'm pretty sure was an astonished expression.

"You're in a big hurry," I commented. "Too big to waste time jawing over nothing. He had a glass gut."

"Indeed!" Swft confirmed. "We must hurry to Her Highness's side!"

"Pretty careless of you, General, to go off and leave your baby princess behind. But you knew what you were doing, didn't you? Just another of your cagey maneuvers. I put her in that 'orifice' of yours and she disappeared."

Swft hurried to the nearest wall, groped, and presto! a secret panel opened. Inside, I saw sunlight on a grassy patch among giant trees; old trees with smooth, purplish bark and chartreuse leaves.

"This," Swft announced, "is disaster!" He stuck his pointy face into the opening and slid inside. I was right behind him, and a good thing, too, because the panel closing behind me almost caught my foot.

Swft was out on the grass, bent over almost double, sniffing at the ground. He looked up at me.

"Timing, as I told you, was of the utmost importance, but now—the necessity to change my plan of action in order to recover Her Highness renders all that nugatory."

"Where are we now?" I asked him. It seemed like a nice, peaceful spot, not a part of any line in the Zone.

"This," the rat-like alien told me, as if making an announcement of public interest, "is the Terminal State."

"Is that anything like a state of confusion?" I inquired, with my usual inappropriate impulse to crack a joke. But he took it seriously.

"Quite the contrary," he informed me. "This phase is—or should be—one of perfect entropic parity; no strife, no difficulty can be long sustained at this level. It is the hope of every Ylokk some day to attain to this level of being. To burst in, as we have done, is our ultimate taboo. I adjusted the transfer device to extrapolate along the prime axis— the most likely direction of the Ylokk future, to its ultimate state. I expected to find an idyllic civilization, existing in flawless harmony with its environment. Instead—this: a wilderness. I am undone!"

"Then why'd you do it?" I came back fast, before he started to develop the idea it was all *my* doing.

"I had no choice," he said brokenly—or anyway, his voice cracked on the words. "It is the only phase that affords undoubted access to the phase where you so rudely dumped Her Highness."

"*Some*body must have programmed that orifice of yours," I pointed out, "presumably you. Either you're a blundering fool, or you're still up to something devious. I think you'd better level with me. I hope the kid's all right, but I thought she'd wind up with Smovia, wherever he had gotten to."

"Not quite," Swft demurred. "You see, it was my intention to transfer our little group to a position inside the Palace, by-passing the Two-Law bandits' cordon. I went first in order to alert our friends and to thwart any enemies who might be present at the point of exit. When no one appeared, I came back by the lone route, to find you alone. Most distressing."

"Sure, you thought I'd enjoy seeing my friends disappear into that shoebox, and I'd love being trapped with a yelling baby in a cell with no window. And a minute ago you said—" I let it go.

"I assumed you'd follow directly," he explained. "The actual aperture is sustained for only a fraction of a minisecond, you know."

"No I don't know," I corrected. "And where are Andy and the doc now?"

"That, I fear, will require some study," Swft told me. "They're quite safe, I feel sure; though doubtless somewhat distressed to find themselves adrift in the entropic pool. We'd best retrieve them at once."

"Good idea," I said. "Why didn't *I* think of that?"

He ignored the irony and shook his head in agreement. "We'd best get cracking," he suggested. "One does tend to lose one's sanity if immersed in the Pool for more than a few microseconds." He rummaged inside his overcoat, took out a complicated gadget, and began running some kind of test sequence, I guessed, from the pattern of flashing LEDs on his hand-calculator-cum-remote-control. I went over to observe, enjoying the feel of the springy turf underfoot.

"Somebody's been here recently," I told him. "The grass has been moved lately."

"Of course," he mumbled, deep in his manipulations. "Ah, yes," he said in a satisfied tone. "We—" Before he could finish that, we heard a crackling in the brush, and a young rat-girl of about ten stepped out of the underbrush into the open. I could tell she was female, though I'm not sure just how. She was dressed in a plain white smock-like garment, and had a rather sweet expression on her rodent face. She had only a short snout; she was almost pretty.

"Hello, Uncle Swft," she said, paying no attention to me at first. Then she gave me a shy glance, and her buck-toothed grin was quite charming. She took a quick, impulsive step toward me, and paused.

"You're not Unca Mobie," she said, as if reproving herself. "You're not Candy," she added. "So you're Unca Null!"

"No, dear," I replied, "I'm certainly not candy."

Just then Swft spoke up. "I fear, my good child," he said rather stiffly, for someone talking to a cute little girl, "that I do not recall our meeting. How do you know my name, may I ask?"

"Unca Mobie" (it sounded like) "said you'd come here sometime." That seemed to be that.

Swft looked at me. "Must be a town nearby," he offered. "Child seems well cared for. Her family must live nearby." He looked at her sharply. "Where do you live, little girl?" he asked.

She waved a slim hand. "Here," she said, as if that were obvious.

"Surely you have a house," Swft corrected her. "Your family: where are they?"

"Unca Mobie there," she said, pointing. "He's taking a nap."

"Oh," Swft said, only half sarcastically, "we

wouldn't want to disturb Unca Maybe's nap, would we?"

"No. Unca *Mobie!*" the girl corrected him sharply.

"Let's go meet him," Swft said gruffly, and started past her, back the way she'd come from. She caught at his arm. He flung her off.

I objected, and took her strange little hard-fingered hand. "He's a little upset," I told the girl. "His plans have gone awry." She smiled. Swft gave me a haughty look.

I felt myself start to slip into the curious awe-and-reverence feeling that occasionally afflicted me out here in the Zone, but pushed it back. I realized it was the pressure of the local mind-set tending to displace my accustomed paradigm. Swft was just a lost, bewildered rat, not a great personage persevering in the face of daunting odds. "Take it easy, General," I suggested. "Be nice to the kid. She's as scared as you are."

"You don't understand, Colonel," he told me in a voice that was tight with anxiety, or whatever it was tight with. "We are in a most perilous situation. To be candid, I have attempted an experiment. I have transferred us across the Yellow Line, into the zone of the hypothetical; to a phase not yet realized in the Skein. This"—he paused to look around at the towering forest all around—"is a state of affairs that *would* come into realization, if the vectors implicit in a great victory of the Jade Palace should, as I hope, eventuate, and are permitted to evolve in a virgin matrix—"

I cut that off. "It's your idea of Utopia, is that about right?" I suggested. He shook his head in affirmation.

"No child should be wandering unattended in this howling wilderness," he complained, "the parameters of which are not to be guessed. I have no idea what horrors may lie beyond this forest. Therefore," he continued, "I have, it is clear, missed the target, and deposited us in some Phase yet undreamt of, a phase without causal linkage to the entropic fabric!"

"Sounds bad, General," I remarked. "Every time we try to make a step forward, we slip back two."

"Not quite," he muttered.

"Relax," I advised the general. "This is no 'howling wilderness'; this is a nice stand of virgin timber. The kid obviously lives nearby. Let's go talk to her folks."

Swft was staring at the girl—not really a girl, I had to remind myself: a rat-pup, not human. She glanced at me with an impish expression, and put a ratty hand on Swft's arm.

"Please do as Unca Swft says," she pled. "I know Candy will be glad to see you."

"I wonder," I commented to the general, "how this kid knows your name."

She supplied the answer: "Unca Mobie said when Unca Null came, Unca Swft would be with him."

She turned and stepped back into the shade of the woods. Swft followed her, and I trailed him. It was dark in there among the great trees. There was no real trail, just a slightly trodden-down strip that meandered among the mossy boles. I stepped along briskly so as not to lose contact with Swft.

We kept this up for maybe half an hour and I was getting impatient, when there was a lessening of the gloom, and suddenly we stepped out into full sunlight. It was a clearing, a hundred yards, almost square, with a small cabin—or "hut" might be a more accurate term—with a trickle of smoke coming from a chimney that seemed to be made of clay.

The rat-girl was at the door already, and Swft drew back, staying in the shadows. I did, too. The girl was still tapping on the door; it opened suddenly, and an old rat—no, a man, thin and whiskered—stood there. He grabbed her and pulled her inside.

I started across to the rescue, but Swft spoke up. "Wait, Colonel. I think it's all right."

"That old devil grabbed her!" I protested. "Probably hasn't seen a female in years!"

"A female of the Noble Folk would hardly be of prurient interest to a humong," he pointed out. I had to concede that, and slowed to a walk.

Swft fell in beside me. "Colonel Bayard," he said, sounding formal, or in some mood that made him speak my name solemnly. "Colonel," he repeated, "I fear you are about to be confronted with a shocking phenomenon. Brace yourself for a surprising revelation."

The old man reappeared in the doorway. "Sure, I'm all set," I replied casually. "But how the devil did a human get *here*?"

"He passed across an entropic discontinuity," Swft told me, as if he knew. "This resulted in a temporal reduplication—"

"Sure." I cut him off. "Skip all that part and get directly to the big surprise."

The old—or at least middle-aged—fellow in the doorway was staring at me as if—I don't know "as if" what. Anyway, he brushed past the little rat-girl and sort of stumbled up to me.

"Colonel," he said clearly, in spite of a frog in his throat, and then lapsed into what sounded like the high-pitched Ylokk speech. But Swft didn't seem to understand any better than I did.

"*Tala sakta,*" Swft said, in Swedish: he'd been

cagey about that one. *"Var god och lysna,"* he added, meaning "Shut up and listen."

I was studying the haggard man's face, which seemed slightly familiar, somehow. He had unevenly hacked whiskers, and deep lines around his eyes, which were blue, and sort of reminded me of—

"Candy! Candy!" Minnie was repeating, tugging at his hand.

" 'Unca Andy,' " I said, trying out the sound. Then, "Lieutenant Helm! Report!"

The old fellow tried to straighten out of his slouch and almost succeeded. He got his mouth closed and brought his right arm up in what I guess was a try at a hand salute. "Colonel Bayard," he croaked, "sir, I have the honor to report that Doctor Smovia is safe and well."

"Unca Mobie!" Minnie yelped, and ran into the hut. I just then realized what I'd decided to call her. Disney never drew a rat.

I took Andy's arm, which was wirier than I remembered it.

"What's happened, Andy?" I asked him.

There were tears in his eyes now. "It really *is* you, sir!" he blurted, and turned and blundered back inside. "Finally!" he added as he disappeared.

"I warned you, Colonel," Swft said. I nodded, and followed Helm into the dim interior. A fire on a stone hearth shed a faint and flickering glow on a bare interior of peeled logs, and Helm bending over a cot where another battered middle-aged man was lying, twisting his head to watch me come in.

"I can't believe it!" he croaked in English, then in Swedish, *"Jag trår inte!"*

Helm was shushing him, at the same time helping him to sit up. He was gaunt, hollow-cheeked, dressed in a ragged, grayish shirt, but I recognized that fanatical look in his eyes. It was young Doc Smovia.

"What's happened to you fellows?" I burst out, then, in a more controlled tone, "it's been awhile, Doctor. What's happened?"

"We climbed through that hole," Smovia said hesitantly, in English. "We came out in a forest. Reminded me of the foothills north of Stockholm. Nobody there. We yelled and got nothing but echoes. The hole we'd crawled out of was gone. It had been about a three-foot fall, and we walked back and forth through where *something* should have been. Nothing. I make it nine years; the lieutenant says ten. We started by keeping a record of the days, but we lost our tally-board in a fire. Nearly lost the house. We tried counting the seasons, but they seem different here; winters are very mild; perhaps the greenhouse effect is further developed."

"You were entropically displaced," I told him. "Did you fellows build this house?"

"No, we found it here, just as it is, unfinished, empty, abandoned," Andy said. "We found a town nearby. Everybody seemed content, used to make a gala event out of the first day of gathering. We went along; nice in the woods. Then, one day, a bunch of loud-mouthed strangers showed up, began interfering, telling people they didn't have to work anymore."

"At first, people tried to argue with them," Smovia contributed. "Said they enjoyed the gathering; but the gangs ridiculed them, said they didn't need to be slaves anymore, that there'd be plenty of new slaves. We got out. We found food in the woods," he continued, "nuts and berries and mushrooms. But we needed more. We killed a small animal—like a squirrel, or maybe a marmoset. Agile little devils. Took a week, but finally we snared one. Built a fire and cooked it. I had some ether in my kit; that helped get the fire started. Delicious! We've eaten pretty well, but, Colonel, it's been a *long* time. Andy looks . . ." He shifted to a lower tone. "—and I do too, I suppose. A pond makes a poor mirror. You have to disturb it to get in position to see your reflection, and . . ." He fell silent and reached out a callused hand to touch my arm. "You're *really* here?" he asked anxiously. "This isn't just another delusion?"

"I'm as really here as anything I know," I told him. "Take it easy, boy. We'll get you out of here."

"They arrested the doc and me," Andy put in. "They left poor Baby—she was about three—to shift for herself. After a few days, some of the locals came with Baby, and let us out. We kept out of sight of the gangs, and sneaked out of town, and after a few days we found the house. We had to fix it up a little, and we had sort of resigned ourselves, I guess. Do you really think we can get back home?"

"We had some doozies," Smovia was mumbling, talking to himself. "Delusions, I mean. Once we saw a parade," he went on. "Big animals, like elephants, only with shovel-tusks, with gold, purple trappings, and rats in blue uniforms and other rats in red on green—"

"The Imperial Guard," Swft said. "The Three Brigades. A state review. How—?"

"Once a party of rats came close to us, halooing and beating the brush," Helm said.

"We thought they were looking for us," Smovia added, "but they passed by and paid no attention to the smoke coming out of the chimney, so it must have been something else."

"Not necessarily," I speculated. "They may have been in another phase, and couldn't see the house."

"Doubtful," Swft supplied. "Although these Two-Law people have taken over the technical complex, they have no one trained in its use."

"That's one for our side," I contributed.

The old fellows had their heads together, discussing something with quiet intensity. Then Helm—I found it hard to think of this haggard middle-aged man as pink-cheeked Lieutenant Helm—went to the little girl-rat and said hesitantly, "Your Highness . . ." He didn't seem to know what to say next. She threw herself at him, embraced him and started to cry. "Candy! Candy! I got losted and . . ." She paused to look at me. "—and Uncanul found me!"

Helm seemed too flustered to speak, and Smovia gently disengaged the girl's grip and hugged and petted her. It seemed she usually spoke Swedish, which was considerably better than her rather babyish English. That wasn't surprising, considering that she'd been raised by a couple of Swedes.

"There, Baby, we're all together now," Helm comforted her. "It's all right—and we'll soon have you home again, now that Uncle Colonel is here."

16

It took a few minutes to get settled and pull homemade chairs up to the slabs-with-the-bark-on table and to get everybody calmed down enough to talk sense—or what had to pass for sense in a milieu devoid of familiar certainties.

"So you two bachelors raised Baby from a pup," I commented. "I'd say you did a good job; she's a nice kid."

"I must protest," Swft put in, not very heatedly. "You must show respect for Her Highness."

"We'll have to skip all that for now, General," I told him. "What do you make of the situation?"

"From the disruption of conditions in the Skein," he stated, "I must conclude that on this once-sacrosanct phase, the Two-Law people have prevailed, and the Noble House has fallen. The Jade Palace is in the hands of its enemies. Now," he went on without pause, "it appears obvious that we must penetrate the City and the Royal Enclosure itself, and after proper preparation, present Her Highness to the populace as proof of the deception on which those Two-Law folk have based their usurpation."

"Swell," I commented. "I hope you have it all worked out just how we're going to do that—and *why* we humongs should stick our necks out."

"To put an end to the invasion," Smovia answered my question. "It's in our interest to restore the old regime, even if it didn't deserve to be preserved for its own sake."

"By which you imply that it does," I interpreted. "Deserve to be preserved, I mean. Tell me why."

"We've told you about the town," Andy put in. "Used to be a nice place: well-tended cottages with fruit trees all around, and the people lived well, and peacefully. Then this Grgsdn bunch came along with their dopey Two-Law propaganda, and everybody became dissatisfied and began to quarrel over the distribution of the town's food supply. It all seemed to devolve on the continuity of the Noble House. With no heir, there'd be no Governance to see to an equitable distribution. The whole system was based on mutual confidence in the honesty of the other fellow, and the idea of "something for nothing" was like a slow poison: everybody was still eating well, but they started to worry, afraid somebody else was slacking on the job, but getting more than his share. Now everybody's starving, and the Killing came, and now it's chaos: a few hundred survivors of the three thousand villagers before the Two-Law business started, all divided into factions, each group embattled in its own little precinct, all concentrating on grabbing what they can of somebody else's harvest, and no relief in sight. There are still organized troops in the capital, but the Governance seems paralyzed; most of the Royal officials refuse to cooperate with Grgsdn, and he can't kill them, because without them, what little order that remains would collapse."

"What makes you think the mere existence of a child heiress will make any difference?" was my next question. Swft and Smovia both spoke at once.

"The people are basically loyal to the old order—"

"These are decent folks: they've just lost their bearings. Once they see a clear path of duty, they'll follow it." Smovia said that, and Swft let it stand.

"First," Andy contributed, "we need to get the rumors started that Grgsdn kidnapped the princess and held her in captivity, and she's just now escaped."

I looked at Minnie, or Baby, or Her Highness as Swft would have it. "What do you think, dear?" I asked her. She gave me that impish grin.

"I think it would be lovely to be a real princess," she told me. She looked warmly at Helm. "Candy told me all about a place called Oz, and about Princess Ozma. I want to be like her."

"I can't blame you for that, my child," I told her. "But we don't have any magic. All we have is science."

"No problem," Smovia spoke up. "Science can do everything magic was ever supposed to do, and more." He stood, a wiry, aging fellow with scraggly whiskers and a light in his eyes.

"Let's do it!" he urged. "I want to see these

people free and happy again, and I want to live to see Baby wearing regal robes, too!"

"It appears to be the most effective way to end the invasion," I conceded without enthusiasm.

"The *only* way!" Swft supplied. "I have hesitated to tell you, Colonel, but Grgsdn has a scheme to open hundreds of new transfer depots and to overwhelm your world with an innumerable horde. That plan must be stopped before it comes to fruition!"

"You haven't told me how it happens that our friends here experienced nine long years while you and I passed only a few hours," I told Swft. He twitched his nose.

"You must understand, Colonel," he said as if the words tasted bad in his mouth, "that the synchronicity of events is a variable not yet completely understood."

"How much time has passed at home while we've been fumbling our assignment out here in the boondocks?"

"I haven't the remotest idea," Swft told me as if scoring a point. "The displacement is dependent on a number of variables, none of which has been controlled. It might be a moment—or a century."

I thought of Barbro and Manfred—all the people I loved—all dead of old age long ago.

"Perhaps no discrepancy at all, of course," Swft was rambling on. "We can only wait and see."

We made our preparations to set out at dawn. They didn't amount to much: just packing up a few days' rations, mostly a kind of pemmican made of pounded nuts and berries and a little squirrel-meat—pretty good as hard rations. We added fresh stuff from the supply bins filled by the old boys, while talking about how to spring Baby's identity on the villagers. We decided that Swft would play her father or guardian, and we humongs—humans; Swft had stopped calling us monkeys a long time ago—would be his captives, brought in from the New Province as technical experts—long live the Two-Laws! We were turncoats, freely cooperating out of of sheer sympathy for the Noble Folk. We'd keep Smovia's vaccine in reserve at first. And I had my vial of the pure virus well-hidden in my belt-box.

The road, such as it was, that ran north toward town ran only a few rods from the hut. We settled down to a steady two miles per hour. Helm and Smovia, in spite of their starved look, were both tough and in condition, and I let them set the pace. Baby kept up with no trouble, and had energy enough left over to make side excursions into the fields to pick wildflowers, which she presented to Unca Mobie, who fashioned them into a wreath with which he crowned her. She laughed and danced along beside us, as carefree as a ten-year-old ought to be.

We came upon a little group of Ylokk emerging from the woods. They halted and conferred when they saw us. Swft told us to look submissive and otherwise ignore them. One of the strangers came toward us, did a complicated head-ducking number, and spoke to Swft. He barked a one-syllable answer and turned to snarl at us:

"These are Two-Law scum. They want to know what you are. I told them to tend to their duties. Play up to me, hurry on, now!" He cuffed Smovia, who crouched, miming terror.

"Don't try that on *me*, Rat!" Helm snapped. I told him to shut up and look subservient. He tried, and succeeded in looking as if he had a bellyache.

I saw a movement in the woods off to the left ahead, and a man—not a rat—pushed out into view. He was a big, beefy fellow with a mean expression. There was another smaller man behind him, then a woman. They carried baskets filled with fat red berries and other stuff. All three humans were youngish and well-dressed—or had been. Their clothes were torn and dirt-stained, and their faces hadn't been washed or shaved lately. The woman's hair was done up in a scraggly knot with a stick through it. The first man seemed to notice us—or the departing Ylokk—suddenly, and ducked back, waving the others back, too. They didn't go far, just about half out of sight.

We watched the rats. We were strung out on the road, but the ragged people paid no attention to me or the other two men—but didn't let Swft out of their sight, ducking around intervening trees and shrubbery to keep him in view. For his part, the General acted as if he hadn't noticed them, but I wasn't fooled. He was too sharp to miss all that play-acting right in front of him.

"Who are they?" I asked him. He did a little, "Eh, what's that?" number and turned to stare after the departing bank of Ylokk, now a hundred yards away down the road. "I told you," he said.

I waved that away. "Don't kid me, Swft," I urged.

It was his turn to pooh-pooh me. "Bands of the rascals roam freely," he said, sounding sad. I grabbed his arm and pointed to the "hiding" humans. He turned on me fiercely. "I told you, Colonel, you must conduct yourself with circumspection!"

"I'm going to talk to them, General," I said. I told Smovia and Andy to stay put, and in spite of

Swft's objection went over to the three people, who were staring at me with blank expressions.

"Here," the burly fellow blurted. "What—?" The woman nudged him and he subsided, looking indignant.

"Hi," I greeted them. "What's happening? I just got here. It looks as if you've had a rough time."

Face to face, the men's whiskers looked like about a week's growth. I had a feeling they'd been in the woods the whole time. Their hands were rough, callused and chapped, with dirt engrained in the pores and under the clipped nails.

"*M'sieur*," the big fellow said carefully, and took a hard grip on my arm.

"*C'est dangereus*," I think he said. He spoke French, but with a Swedish accent. He was urging me toward the nearest clump of underbrush, questioning me urgently, I gathered, and he kept glancing toward Swft.

"That's General Swft," I told him. That was all I thought he'd understand. If he did, he didn't show it.

"Who *are* you people?" I insisted. He seemed to confirm the assumption of English-speaking tourists everywhere: that anybody could understand plain English, if spoken loudly enough. The ragged fellow frowned and said in badly-accented English:

"Like you—slaves."

Swft came over and told me sternly, "You can't fraternize with these trash."

"They're people, like me," I told him. "What are they doing here? How did they get here?"

The three strangers seemed intimidated by Swft; they drew back, watching him closely, especially the big guy. Swft kept his distance and told me, in

Swedish, to get back on the road and ignore these people. He kept glancing off toward the band of Ylokk, almost out of sight around a bend. "Hurry!" he urged me.

Smovia and Andy had come over and were talking excitedly to the strangers. Helm knew French well—or at least he talked fast—and Big Boy seemed to understand him. He turned to me. "They're slaves, Colonel," he told me. So much for linguistic facility. I nodded, and asked the woman how they'd got here. She replied that they'd walked out from town, "as usual."

"I mean to this A-line," I amplified, impatiently.

"In a big box," the smaller man spoke up. "The rats jumped us—Marie and me—back in Göteborg and herded us inside a big lift-van, and held us for two days—along with ten other people they'd waylaid on the street. Then they opened a door and we came out—here. Gus came along the next day."

17

I interrogated them further and was told they wondered where they were; it didn't look like any part of Sweden they knew of. They came to the woods every day to gather berries, truffles, nuts, and something else I didn't understand. The bruiser was named Gus, and the other fellow Ben. Marie was the woman, and Gus acted as if he owned her, but she seemed to prefer Ben.

Swft was dithering all the while we talked, and I finally turned to him. "Things are beginning to be a little clearer, Swft. You're still being cagey. The 'invasion' is actually a slave-raid, isn't it?"

"Why, as to that," he temporized, managing a passable shrug with his short arms, "there was some talk of recruitment, not that I personally approved the idea . . ."

"Don't kid me," I told him. "You already let slip that labor was the big problem at the root of all your troubles. The Two-Law folks don't believe in work, you said, and the Jade Palace people are above all that. So—once you discovered an intelligent, non-Ylokk species, it seemed your troubles were over. Right so far?"

"It wasn't—" he tried to butt in.

I rolled right over that. "You were wrong. They were just beginning. Now the Imperium knows where you are, and *what* you are, so it seems you goofed—badly."

"Still," Swft put in coldly, "you humans are here, alone among us, and quite dependent on me for your lives, to say nothing of return to your own phase to report your mistaken ideas."

"Don't count on it," I said, but I knew he was right.

"That party of constabulary," he went on, "would have shot you down out-of-hand, had I not told them you were of my personal retinue."

"You're a big-hearted guy," I told him sardonically.

"As for these—" he went on, indicating the three newcomers, "they're escaped workers, under sentence of slow dismemberment. Unless you wish to be included in that fate, you'll shun them. Those Two-Law vermin were not quite satisfied. Even now, they're holding a parley just down the road. They could well return. And if they do . . ." He left the rest to the imagination. I glanced down that way. He was right: they were just falling back into ranks, facing our way.

"Quickly!" Swft hissed. "Back into the woods!" I decided to go along, because those ten Ylokk cops definitely had that "All right, this is a pinch" look on their snouty faces.

The three escaped slaves went along readily: it seemed probable that it was them the cops were looking for in the first place. Swft wanted us to scatter and hide, but Helm said, "Colonel, what about an ambush instead?"

"Nonsense!" Swft interposed. "We've none of those clever lead-throwers of yours."

"Glass guts," Helm countered. "We lie low, and take 'em one at a time; there's seven of us against ten; fair odds."

"Let's do it," I agreed.

Smovia protested a little, but cooperated readily enough.

"We let them all pass, and pick off tail-end Charlie," I told them. "I'll take the first one, then you get the next fellow, Andy." The new people were enthusiastic. I put them last, followed up by Swft, who agreed to talk to the leader, a fellow with a light-blue stripe down his back. I told Baby to hide and stay put.

The Ylokk came crashing into the brush, talking back and forth. One straggler paused to pump ship uncomfortably close. I let him finish, then came up fast and drove a good stiff right jab to his short ribs. He folded, making only a few whistling sounds. Andy took his rat out right on cue, and old Gus looked pretty good, handling his boy and then Smovia's, while Ben and Marie together felled a couple more. I went up fast and intercepted two rats trying to make a run for it, and laid them out left and right. They seemed to be unarmed except for nightsticks they didn't try to use. It was over in about a minute and a half.

"This is fun," Andy said. "It looks like we won't have much trouble here."

"These spiritless dupes are not representative of the Noble Folk," Swft was quick to correct him.

"We must take care to secure the alliance of the Loyalists, and not to antagonize them."

"That ought to be easy," I supplied, "considering that we're here to help them overthrow the revolt."

"You must be careful to make the distinction," Swft counseled.

Gus drew me and Helm aside to demand why a Ylokk was fighting on our side. I explained that he was a representative of the Old Order and that he opposed the Two-Law faction that had captured the Jade Palace.

"These fellows," Andy indicated the ten fallen Ylokk, "are some of the ones we told you about. They just showed up one day. That's why we left town. Who *are* they? What are they after?"

"They're a bunch who think the world owes them a living," I tried to explain. "They reject the Third Law of Motion—"

"That's the one that says you don't get something for nothing, right?" Andy asked, nodding to confirm his suggestion. I agreed.

"That's crazy," Smovia contributed. "You can't repeat a law of Nature. But you know, I've met people like that at home!"

"These fellows think you can," I told him, "by capturing enough slaves to do all the work."

"That explains a lot," Ben said. "What are we doing about it? What *is* this place? How did we get here? That box they packed us in—"

"How many of you were there?" I wanted to know.

"Twenty-one in my bunch," Ben replied. "And a lot more bunches. There's no real use in fighting back."

"In Stockholm, we've got them on the run," I

told him. "They're not much as soldiers. They're sick."

" 'The Killing,' " Smovia supplied. "They started dying just about the time the gangs showed up. Terrible."

"Maybe they're responsible," it occurred to me. "Their kind think that things like garbage and sewage disposal just happen; they've probably let things go to pot and contaminated the water supply."

"Quite right, Colonel," Swft put in. "These moronic upstarts have kept the power-generating plant in operation by holding the former staff by force. They seem amazed when the employees come to them for instruction as to how to handle emergencies. They reply indignantly, 'I'm the *boss*! I don't bother with such matters! That's *your* job!' "

"No wonder things fell apart," I commented. I tried to explain to Gus that he and the others had been transferred from their native A-line to a distant one. He brushed that aside.

"Is there some way to get *back*?" Ben demanded. I told him that we intended to retake the Skein Technical Compound, and after putting an end to Ylokk transfers to the Zero-zero line, and with Swft's help, to use their equipment to return all the captives home.

"What are we waiting for?" he wanted to know.

"First," I explained, "we have to take over the little town, and recruit a force of Ylokk opposed to the Two-Lawers—"

"Impossible!" Gus snapped.

"That'll be easy," Ben contradicted. "Everybody hates them. All they need is some leadership, to throw all of them into their own slave pits."

"How many humans are there in the town?" was my next question.

"Maybe a few hundred," Gus guessed. "They come and go. The place is a sort of staging area for breaking in the new arrivals to the system. Show 'em how to go to the woods and gather stuff, and all. And to break 'em down so they give up and forget dumb ideas about trying to escape. Where's there to escape to? This is a foreign country, even though it's the same geography as home.

"What do we do with these bums?" Gus demanded, looking hungrily at our captives. He had a carving knife in his hand. "Cut their throats?" he suggested, taking a step toward the nearest as if he assumed the answer was yes.

Instead I said, "No, we use them."

"Use 'em how?" Andy almost demanded before he heard what he'd said, and mumbled, "Use 'em. Yessir."

"Ease off on the Prussian discipline, Andy," I ordered him. "We're in this together. Take it easy."

"How," Swft cut in, "do you propose to 'use' these miscreants? I cannot, of course, stand by while atrocities are performed."

"You don't have a whole lot to say about it, General," I reminded him. "First, get them on their feet; then pull rank on them and tell them they're your escort. Get them cleaned up a little."

"Then what?" Gus demanded.

"The less I hear from you, right now, Gus-baby," I told him, "the better I'll like you." He muttered but shut up and rejoined Marie, who edged away from him. She gave me a tentative smile and I said, "Ma'am, for the present I'd like you to pretend that the incompetents have captured all of us, and that General Swft is in charge. Do as he says, please."

I turned to Swft. "We're going into town," I told him. "You'll be able to find slave-quarters for us, and a good meal for the troops. We'll trade with them."

"I foresee no difficulty," he acknowledged, and barked something peremptory at the nearest fallen Ylokk, the one with the blue back-stripe, who was just getting his feet under him. He glanced up at Swft and cringed back and snarled something that didn't sound like "Yessir." Swft nudged him with his foot and said something in a quiet but deadly tone. The sergeant scrambled up and immediately grabbed Andy's arm. Andy knocked him on his back. Swft said, "None of that, wretched humong!" Andy swung on Swft, who blocked the haymaker casually and said into Helm's teeth,

"You'd best play along, Lieutenant, if you hope to survive the day. The others are at hazard, too."

"*Djäveln!*" Helm spat. "We've already shown these rats who's in charge!"

"We can't beat the entire garrison, Andy," Swft told him. "They've no doubt called for reinforcements. In a few moments, we'll be surrounded by two hundred trained policemen."

Andy looked at me.

"You heard the general," I told him. "You also heard me, I think. We're under cover, Lieutenant, passing as slaves. Get with the program." He complied reluctantly.

The sergeant—his name turned out to be Dvd—was back on his feet, sounding indignant. Swft barked a command at him and went on to the next Ylokk. It took him ten minutes to get them all in line, with the sergeant's assistance; then he held a

conference with the non-com and left him to shape
up the detail in a column of twos. By that time, we
could see Ylokk out on the road, standing at the
ready, while their OIC talked into a hand-held
talker. Swft said, "Wait here, if you will, Colonel,"
and went over toward them. They came to a sloppy
alert, but snapped-to when they got a good look at
that red stripe. He had a short talk with the captain and turned to yell back to Sergeant Dvd,
"Bring them out."

Dvd rather sheepishly gestured to me to fall in,
and at my request, Gus, Ben and Marie lined up,
and Smovia, Helm and I got in place beside them.
Baby was talking to a cop with a bloody nose, and
gave him a hanky to wipe it. Dvd got his boys back
in a row and gave the "move out" signal. We
dutifully shuffled out into the sunlight, trying to
look like homeless chattels who were sorry they'd
ever run away. The captain bought it. He could
see the signs of a struggle, but had no way of
knowing who'd won it, except the lies Swft was
telling him.

". . . attempted to resist," the general was saying.
"I explained to the sergeant that I required these
humongs for my own work, and . . ."

I brought our little band to a foot-shuffling halt
and looked at Dvd, as if for orders.

"Colonel, we can take this bunch, too," Helm
muttered to me. "There's only twenty-four of 'em.
Let me—"

"You'll receive your instructions, Lieutenant," I
whispered back. "Maybe a little of that Prussian
discipline would be in order after all."

Swft turned to snap an order at Dvd, who turned
hard on me and squealed, "Silence!" We silenced.

Swft went over and spoke quietly to Baby; then

he took one of the long overcoats from one of the smaller cops, and helped her into it. That was a good idea; now she could mix with the troops and look unexceptional. We moved closer to the newly-arrived Ylokk, trying to discourage them from looking too closely at the row of sheepish-looking Ylokk ostensibly guarding us. Swft was tête-à-tête with the captain. After a brief conference, the latter motioned his NCOIC over and gave him orders. The new squad fell in and right-faced and went around us into the woods and began pushing our captives around.

Swft objected sharply. The captain gave orders and in a moment the two groups were lined up side by side. Swft came over and told me, "I told Captain Fsk to place these fellows under arrest," he notified me. "Insubordination," he explained, "and incompetence."

"These reinforcements don't seem very motivated," I commented. "Whose side are they on?"

"They're not quite sure, actually," Swft confided. "They're trained regulars, and are hesitant to take orders from these newly-arrived gangs of ne'er-do-wells; they recognize my rank, and so far that's been enough to keep them off balance. I told them it's an Imperial exercise; they are, after all, under my command, and I'm playing it by ear. Please continue to cooperate, Colonel, and we may bring this off yet."

18

After a considerable amount of confusion and some vocal disagreements among the rank and file, Captain Fsk got the whole bunch in line, four abreast, grumbling abreast, grumbling but obedient.

"Move out, Captain," Swft ordered, and urged us slaves ahead.

We dutifully took our position, but Gus commented, "I hope we're not being suckered, Colonel. I don't trust these damn squirrels, *none* of 'em!" He was looking hard at Swft.

"General Swft is dedicated to the overthrow of the group that's backed the invasion," I told him. "Actually, it's a slave-raid, rather than a true invasion."

"When I see them damn squirrels pushing people off the sidewalk," he returned hotly, "and strutting in to take all the tables at my favorite café, I call it an invasion."

"What do you want, Gus?" I asked him. "To put an end to the invasion, or just show off what a hell of a man you are?"

"Run 'em out," he conceded. "If play-acting will help, I'll do it."

"You sure will," I confirmed. We were catching a bad smell from up ahead. We shuffled along in silence, and in a few minutes we saw masonry houses looming above trimmed trees, and came into the edge of what should have been a pleasant little town. The street was lined with tall, shabby masonry buildings with broken windows and missing cornices. But the dead were everywhere: lying on the walks and in the streets, stacked in alleys. It looked as if at first there had been some attempt to pile them up neatly, but later they'd just thrown them into heaps. Bones, mostly, but enough fresh corpses to show the Killing was still active. As I watched, a body fell from a high window, impacted in the street, and lay anonymously among the others.

I saw a feeble movement in a nearby pile. Someone was alive in there and trying to get out. I took an automatic step in that direction, but Swft caught my arm. "Colonel," he said stiffly, "we have no time for kindly gestures."

I felt an impulse to apologize, but I realized I was being influenced by the local paradigm; so I gave Swft a fierce look, and said, "I understand the needs of this force, General."

A Ylokk came out of a shop that looked like small shops look everywhere. He glanced up, saw us, and let out a screech, as if he'd just discovered the town was on fire. Other rats appeared, forming up in a crescent-shaped barrier. Swft spoke to the captain; he barked an order and his troops hurried up to form up in two columns alongside us six "prisoners." Swft came over and told me this was disgraceful; that the interference of the Two-Law squads had so far destroyed civil order that the mob felt it was appropriate to interfere with what was clearly an official detail guarding captive humongs. He stamped away to confront the still-gathering crowd and to deliver a short, deadly-sounding speech. The excited townsfolk began to drift away.

Then two burly, wharf-rat types pushed through to the front rank. One of them pointed at Andy, and both of them started toward him. Swft ordered them to stay clear. They ignored him. He waited until they were abreast of him, and abruptly bent forward, swinging his long torso sideways, and whipped it around, knocking both the trouble-makers off their feet. A few of the crowd seemed to object, but most of them yelled something equivalent to "Bravo!" Swft went over and yanked the bigger of the two to his feet and spat words in his face, then threw him aside. The other scuttled away, yapping over his narrow shoulder at the mob as they parted to let him through.

"He'll fetch the rest of the garrison," Swft said. "I need to get you people out of sight, Colonel."

That suited me. The muttering crowd was in a lynch mood; they just weren't sure whom to lynch: the hated gang who had intruded on their peaceful lives, the representative of the old and presumably discredited order, or the humongs. We followed Swft's gestures into a dim-lit interior, while he formed his bunch into a defensive square, covering the doorway. The townspeople were rapidly dispersing. Swft joined us inside what appeared to be a restaurant, and gave orders to a scared-looking old rat with a gray-tipped pelt. We sat down on the too-low benches and in a moment a young ratess put long wooden trenchers full of some kind of stew in front of us. It smelled neutral.

"This is good, wholesome food," Swft assured us as he dipped in. Baby picked tentatively at hers, then nodded—she had her head-gestures right— and said, *"Det ar bra, Farbro Swft."* I tasted mine: it seemed to be a sort of mushroom-and-nut goulash, not bad. While we ate, the noises outside developed into a full-fledged crowd-roar whipped along by the shrill yelps of the Two-Law boys. They seemed to be preparing for an assault on the restaurant. I asked Swft what he had in mind next.

"I promised you safe conduct," he told me. "You shall have it." A window shattered as a rock sailed through and thumped on the floor. The host, all atwitter, hurried outside, squeaking, and staggered back a moment later, bleeding. Swft went to the entry, paused for a moment, and went out, to be confronted by the front rank of the noisy mob. He knocked a few of them aside, and said, as well as I could interpret:

"Those who would interfere with me and my troops, in defiance of peace and order, and of the law of the Governance, will very soon discover the error of their ways. You will ignore the impertinent intruders who are urging you to disorder, and return to your usual tasks. I shall deal with the rabble-rousers in just and dispassionate fashion. Now go!"

A short but burly rat charged him, to be met with a snap of Swft's jaws that sent him back, bleeding from a nasty bite on his stubby forearm. Two more tried and were felled by Swft's snappy torso-sweep. The townspeople were churning around uncertainly, waiting to see who was going to win. More of the Two-Law bullies came out of a side street at a run, swept around the crowd, and began to close in from both sides. Swft stepped back inside and confronted me. "You see the situation, Colonel. Our social order is badly disturbed. Ordinarily, one word from me would have been enough to disperse this crowd—and as for the Two-Law trash—pah!" He caught my eye. "You *must* get Her Highness through to safety, Colonel!" He was sounding desperate. "I've spoken to Captain Fst, and you may rely on him, insofar as his small command can help you."

He turned to Baby then. "Highness," he said. "I return now to my duty. Pray put your reliance in Colonel and his humongs." Then he turned and went back outside. The mob noise rose even higher, and I heard the unmistakably meaty *thud!* of a rock hitting flesh. I saw Swft recoil, turn slowly, and fall sideways. The crowd surged over him. That seemed somehow to defuse them, or bring them to their senses. They drew back from Swft's body, leaving a pitiful heap in the street. A Two-Law thug started to yell something, and was at once knocked down. The townspeople were moving back and away, disappearing down the side street whence they had come. Swft's body looked very lonely out there on the cobbles.

"*Djäveln!*" Andy said at last. Smovia was comforting Baby, who was babbling about "Unca Swft." The host appeared, looking anxious, and I shunted him into a corner, just as he was darting back into his hutch at the back of the room.

He dithered, then decided to be cooperative. "You fools!" he snarled. "You'll get us all killed!"

"Whose side are you on?" I demanded.

He tried to duck past me, and yelled "guard!"

He was looking to Baby in her cop-coat for help.
She was busy.

I pushed him back into the corner. "That was
Lieutenant General Lord Swft they murdered out
there," I told him. "He was fighting for the outster
of these hoodlums and a return to peace and order. Where do you stand?"

"The vandals broke in here, and robbed my
larder," he whined. "Where are the troops of Her
Majesty?"

"Why didn't you throw them out?" I demanded.

"They were many and I was alone," he moaned.
"What could I do?"

"If the whole town had united against them," I
pointed out, "you could have locked them all in
the local dungeon."

"But there were many who hoped to profit," the
innkeeper complained. "I saw them, just now,
standing by outside, while the Two-Laws killed
your friend, eager to take a share of the loot."

"Are you willing to do something now?" I asked
him. "It's not too late to take your town back."

"What?" he was yelping. "What can we do now?
All order is fled, peace is a forgotten fancy. They
lord it over us all, treat us as mere slaves—oh, beg
your pardon, sir."

"It's all right," I told him. "We're not slaves.
These troops here are *our* prisoners—those that
aren't on our side."

"But you can't— Why did they stand by and
allow—" He became incoherent—not that I was
an expert on colloquial—and hysterical—Ylokk di-
alect, anyway.

"What are we going to do now, sir?" Helm
wanted to know. "With the general dead, how—?"

"First we're going to get his body in here: show

the respect he's earned. Then we'll have to get into the city and inside the Skein technical compound," I told him.

Doc Smovia was at the door, checking the chance of getting to Swft's body. "I think the troops should bring him in, Colonel," he said.

"Tell Captain Fsk to break the square, send two men after Swft, and retreat inside," I instructed.

Smovia relayed the message then growled, "What about those Two-Law bastards? And when do I get to start my epidemiological work? These people are *sick*."

"As soon as we've dealt with the rebels," I replied.

"We need to do our work here and get home!" Smovia burst out.

"Damn right!" Gus blurted. His fat face was flushed.

The troops came in carrying Swft carefully and squeaking excitedly.

Baby threw herself into the group crying, "He's alive! He's alive!"

Smovia immediately started issuing orders and clearing the way for an examination. "Andy! Take Baby and try to keep her calm," was the only thing he said for a while. Then, "I think he'll live. He's going to need a kind of care I'm not sure we can provide."

"Do the best you can," I told him. "The general almost gave his life for us. We owe him something."

"Damn rat town," old Gus contributed.

I'd had enough of his big mouth. I put a fist in it and told him if I heard any more unsolicited advice out of him I'd have to do it again, only harder.

He was rubbing his jaw and then looking amazed at the blood on his hand. "Got no call," he started.

I made a shoving motion. "Stand in the corner and shut up," I ordered him.

Smovia started to interfere, but Andy shushed him.

Gus turned to Ben. "He's gonna sell us to the rats—" he babbled. Helm spun him around and socked him in the belly, then shoved him into the corner.

The innkeeper was dithering as he listened, uncomprehending, to our discussion in English.

I summoned my patchy knowledge of the Ylokk language and asked him if he'd decided where he stood. He gulped and said, "By the side of Right! If you strange beings intend to attack these ruffians, I'm with you."

I congratulated him and asked him if he'd care to start by provisioning us for our expedition into the capital and arranging for the care of Swft.

"Oh, better than that, sir!" he was eager to assure me. "I have the honor to place at your disposal my conveyance, with myself as conductor! They know me well in the city. I, Bnk, am, by appointment, purveyor to the Jade Palace of fresh provender daily—except that these scum have prevented me, these two weeks now. Come, I shall show you my equipage." I followed the old fellow out back and dutifully looked at a sagging two-wheeled cart, lacking only a broken-down plow-horse to be a perfect picture of inadequate transportation.

"Still," Smovia said behind me. "Presuming there's a draft animal, it's better than walking. Our blisters could become septic, if we don't tend them soon. And it will allow us to keep Swft immobile while he recovers."

"Sure," I agreed. "We'll accept," I told Bnk. As

soon as we could get the cart loaded with whatever he normally delivered to the Palace, we'd be ready to go. He took us back inside and showed us which bales and kegs to load up. Smovia fixed up the space for Swft, and I set Gus and Ben to the job while the rest of us stood guard. Gus complained until I rapped him again. He was one of those slow learners. Marie tried to comfort him, but he snarled at her. It seemed she was afraid of him.

"Whatever shall I tell the Lord Chamberlain?" Bnk inquired of a hostile universe.

"Tell him the truth," I suggested.

"And how am I to explain yourselves?" he wanted to know next.

"We'll get under the tarp," I told him.

"Colonel," Andy signed in, "do you really think they'll let us waltz out of here with a load of valuable supplies?"

"Bnk has his rounds to make," I told him, "and they ought to be willing to let him make his delivery to Grgsdn in the Palace. We'll lie low until we're clear of town."

Bnk fetched a strange, hippo-sized, tapir-like animal from a leanto and harnessed it to the cart. It smelled like well-aged barnyard. Bnk was absently patting the dung-caked flank and batting at the big blue flies. There was very little room left in the cart for six people. We could let Minnie ride on the seat with Unca Bnk. She called all adult males "Unca"; she didn't seem to make any distinction between Ylokk and human, but she had kind of taken a shine to Marie, who seemed to reciprocate the attraction. Aside from her tending to baby-talk in English, she seemed like a level-headed ten-year old. But no doubt Smovia and Helm had started off talking baby-talk to her and had gotten used to it, and she naturally learned what she heard.

There was a stiff, smelly tarp with the cart; I arranged it so as to give us full cover but still allow a little breathing, plus a spy-hole for me. I gave Bnk his instructions: to act as if it were a normal delivery, and to expect no interference; if he got any, he was to object loudly and keep going.

19

It was hot, dusty, buggy and stinky as well as crowded under the tarp, and I seemed to be lying on gravel. The big thing, I realized immediately, was not to fidget and not to sneeze. With that settled, I went to sleep.

I awoke to the sounds of high-pitched Ylokk voices, yelling: "—told you no more slave-services to the bloodsuckers!" one harangued.

"—the Folk's food!" another yelped.

Old Bnk was replying spiritedly:

"—shall I not see the needs of the great Grgsdn? He, too, requires nourishment, and his selfless dedication to the Folk allows him no time to forage! Would you have him starve?"

After a little more of this wordplay, the alert guardians of other people's business decided to let him pass. One of them jagged at the tarp with a pole or a spear-butt and gave me a bruise on the shoulder. Then we were bumping along, every jolt driving sharp gravel-bits into my flesh like thumb-tacks. I peeked out through my spy-hole and watched the guard detail recede around a curve.

"OK," I said to the others, "from here we walk awhile."

Fresh air never smelled better. After a few busy minutes of flea-chasing, aided by a bottle of stuff Bnk produced from the box under his seat, we set off in the dusty wake of the cart, enjoying breathing, moving freely, the absence of aged fecal matter, and no pain except for our blisters. This lasted for a good two minutes. Then Bnk halted the cart and made frantic "down" motions.

We took to the ditch and watched until they'd passed, ten of them, dowdy-looking fellows looking more like stragglers than a disciplined squad.

"What do you think, Andy?" I asked the wiry old devil I was still used to thinking of as young Lieutenant Helm. He edged forward to get his face close to my ear. "I want that sucker with the blue stripe," he replied.

"We'll have to take two apiece on the first pass," I said. He nodded. I spoke quietly to Gus and Marie, who insisted she'd like a piece of the action. Doc Smovia was game, if not eager. He put Minnie in back of a bush and told her to stay put.

"We stand up and move *quietly* to the trail," I told them. "I'll take the last two. Andy, you handle the next pair; we have to hit fast and hard."

We selected heavy, two-foot clubs from among the lengths of hard fat pine lying all around. I sneaked out of the fringe of brush and closed in on tail-end Charlie. I didn't do it very well, because he turned around just in time to see the club coming; he ducked, not far enough, and managed a yelp, which the fellow in front of him heard, and that one turned and went down under a solid blow between the eyes. Andy went past me and took his blue-stripe and another one, and then it was free-for-all.

One of the rats tried to run for it, but I tripped him and hauled him upright and took the starch out of him with a short jab to that glass gut.

He was simultaneously snapping at my wrist and trying to say something. Finally I caught a few words: "—three-Law. We're not hunting you, humong! I am Major Lst, and I am of the Loyal Opposition!" He twisted in my grip and yelped at Gus, who was throttling a rat nearby, and bleeding from bites on his bare forearms.

"Mister Guz! It is I, your benefactor, Lst!" He was struggling to free himself, but I held on.

Gus, red-faced and furiously intent on what he was doing, ignored the major, but Ben came over and yelled over the din of screeching rats and cursing men. "—mistake!" he was saying. "These fellows are on *our* side!"

I threw Lst down and put a foot on him. He tried to bite my ankle. I kicked him under his receding chin and said "Naughty!" He stared up at me balefully, then shifted his attention to Ben and started a long, yapping speech I couldn't follow.

Ben said, "Colonel," then interrupted himself to fell Gus with a haymaker. "These fellows are what's left of the royal garrison," he told me. "They oppose the Two-Law scum, of course, and disapprove of the big slave raid. The major here"— he was helping the now passive officer to his feet— "helped us escape. They'll help us get into town to attack the thugs."

I took his word for it when Marie came over and

confirmed what he said, taking his arm posses-
sively, and smiling up at him. She was no beauty,
but she did have a nice smile, and her club had
rat-hair clotted on it. A useful trooper.

"Major Lst unlocked the cell door," she told me
quickly. "At first we didn't trust him; we thought
it was a trick to kill us while 'attempting to escape' or something. But when we saw him club
down the Two-Law captain, we knew he was with
us. After all, he has reason to hate them; I know
he'll help us attack the rebels."

It took a couple of minutes to restore order,
with Lst's boys, a little the worse for wear, lined
up in ragged ranks, and our side, surrounding
them. Smovia got busy disinfecting bites, and then
I let him patch up a few scalp wounds that were
leaking blood into rats' eyes. Andy was the last to
let go; then Smovia reminded him this was the
same bunch they'd seen pass by their cottage in
the woods and ignore it.

Lst spoke up: "I had to make a show of searching for you, after you fled the town," he explained.
"The Two-Laws suspected I'd helped you—as I
indeed had. I reported no sign of you, and then,
later, I helped the other slaves to escape. You may
trust me."

"Do you know General Swft?" I asked him.

"Indeed I have that honor!" he declared. "Have
you seen the general?"

"He's out of the picture at this time," I said.
"He was gravely injured by a mob at the road-
house up the way. We have him with us, but I
don't know how much good that is."

"I had hoped to make contact with the general,"
Lst said. "It was our plan—I speak of the loyalist
troops—to rally on him and retake the capital."

"We can still do it," I told him. "Any ideas?"

"I meant to recruit any escaped slaves I could find, march them back, and then, when the Two-Laws turned out to formally receive the runaways, to fall on them all together," Lst said. "Would you have the general checked and a report of his condition made?"

"Sounds all right to me," I said. I asked Andy and Smovia if they saw any flaw, from what they knew of the situation in town.

Smovia couldn't think of any and went over to check on the general still unconscious in the cart.

"The Two-Laws always make a big thing of parading recaptured slaves," Helm told me. "The whole gang will be there, intent on strutting around, showing how superior they are. Lst is right: that's the time to take them, from both sides at once!" He was so full of enthusiasm that he forgot to apologize for expressing his opinion.

Smovia returned and told me we were on our own for a while, as the general was going to be out of it for a while longer.

I asked Lst if he thought Bnk could get Swft to safety with other loyalist troops, while we carried his plan out.

Lst talked to Bnk for about ten minutes, then assigned two troopers to him and sent them off. He explained to me that there were loyalists on the grounds of the Jade Palace, and that they would be safe there, and have Swft taken care of, by morning.

We withdrew into the woods for a little R and R, prepared to do or die at dawn.

Cheerful old Gus came over and muttered for a while until I told him that if he had something to say, to speak up.

"You ain't trusting these here rats, are you?" he demanded. "I say let's slit their throats while they're asleep."

"You," I told him, "will, by God, shut up and get busy following your orders. I have neither the time nor the inclination to bother with your neuroses, Gus. Go get some sleep and don't hatch any dumb ideas."

After he'd lumbered away, Smovia spoke up: "You could have been a bit more diplomatic, Colonel. Gus is a lout, but we'll need him in a fight."

"Did you notice him during the last fracas?" I asked Doc. "He tackled one fellow and got knocked down. He didn't try again. I think he's as gutless as loudmouths usually are."

Smovia let it go at that. After what seemed like a very short time, Marie woke me for my turn at guard duty. She was cold to the bone and so was I, but we couldn't risk a fire; the Two-Law constabulary would be patrolling the area, Ben assured me. Finally dawn came, and five minutes later we were on the march—not on the road, of course, but following trails Andy showed me. We passed houses, built low and usually partly dug-in, showing neglect. I saw a party of humans in the distance, headed into the woods for another day of doing the Two-Law people's work for them; their Ylokk escort was close on their flank. We lay low until they were well past.

I asked Andy how many slaves were in the town. He estimated fifty. The Two-Law cadre was about the same size. I asked him if he thought the humans would rally to us when they saw what was happening. He was dubious. "They're a long way from home, sir," he explained on their behalf.

"They're apathetic. I managed to talk to a couple of them, but they didn't seem interested."

"I'm wondering," I told him, "why you and Doc weren't pressed into a work gang as soon as you appeared in town."

"We got there ahead of the Two-Law rebels, sir," he told me. "Doc had his kit and he treated a couple of sick pups and they recovered. Their folks protected me from the Two-Laws when they arrived; everybody seemed to know about the slave-raids and they knew we were the species being enslaved, but they didn't approve. They were expecting the Royal Guard to show up at any moment to run the rebels off. They hid us and fed us and treated us as well as they could under the circumstances."

20

Meanwhile, we had things to do. Marie pointed out that we ought to have gathering baskets, and she showed us the kind of grass they were woven of and how to weave them. It took us half an hour, good old Gus bitching all the while.

Baby, or Minnie as we called her about half the time (she liked the name) thought it was all grand fun, and quickly filled her basket with wildflowers, and I had to ask her to dump them and fill it with nuts and berries instead, at Doc's suggestion: the Two-Laws wouldn't take kindly to slaves wasting their time plucking daises. I put her at the end of Major Lst's column. (The name I render "Lst" was actually more like "List," with the first consonant on an indrawn breath, but even he knew who I meant when I said "List." I would never be fluent in Ylokk: too many gasping sounds and squeals.)

Little Minnie, in her soldier's coat, looked enough

like a young male recruit to get by. I told her to take to cover at the first indication of attack. She agreed, but actually I think she had rather enjoyed hitting a bit Two-Law sergeant over the head in our last set-to when he attacked Doc, though she tended him carefully after it was over; now she was his pal, sort of a mascot to the squad. That was good for morale, mine as well as theirs.

The sun was high and warm now. We sweated —we humans, that is—and were glad we didn't have to wear overcoats. The troops didn't seem to mind, even Minnie. Our new escorts were in good spirits; from what I could catch of their conversations in ranks, they expected to wipe up the rebels fast, and proceed to the capital to do the same there.

I warned Lst to keep them under control, with no indiscriminate looting or rough stuff with the citizens. He assured me that their discipline was good, and that he realized we needed the towns-folk as allies.

We saw a small group of Ylokk with shovels, loafing under a tree up ahead. They looked our way and got to their feet as if to interfere.

"Two-Law trash," Lst told me. I told him to form up his boys in a box around us, his supposed captives. When he had done so, he hurried ahead, and one of the loafers moved out as if to intercept him. Lst feinted left, then whipped his torso around like Swft had done and knocked the fellow ten feet, where he lay kicking and gasping. Lst snapped a command at the others, and they sullenly set to work digging a long, narrow grave. Lst gestured and they picked up their erstwhile pal, still wheezing, and threw him in. When the hole was backfilled,

Lst told them to stamp on it, to pack down the loose dirt.

"Pretty rough, wasn't that, Lst?" I suggested.

He showed his incisors in a snarl. "That's all these trash can understand," he stated flatly.

"Hey," Gus spoke up beside me. "Maybe this here rat is OK."

I was still uncomfortable. I told Lst to exhume the living soldier. He complied, complaining. The buried rat came up out of the dirt, clawing his way through the final layers of clods. Suddenly, his old pals were pals again, crowding around him to help dust the dirt from his narrow shoulders.

"Good work, Colonel," Helm said quietly. "Saved me coming back to dig him up before he suffocated."

The congratulatory group and the object of their welcome-back came over to talk to Lst. He interpreted:

"They liked that; say they were really scared old Crt had had it; good to meet an officer who knows how to handle troops. They want to join my command. They suggested we kill all you slaves, just for fun. Especially you, Colonel. I told them I had a job for you: that we're headed for the capital to kick Grgsdn out and restore the good old days. They liked that and wanted to join us. I told them 'all right.' They're enlisted. That makes twenty-six. We're making progress."

"We've been lucky," Lst told me when we were back in formation and moving along if not briskly, at least steadily toward the city we could see now, rising misty beyond the forest. "All these fellows are confused: they're used to taking their orders from the royal commandment; then suddenly the Two-Law people swarmed in and said *they* represented the new law and order. They had to go along, or be killed. Some fellows were beaten to death when they didn't. Now they're still afraid of their Two-Law bosses, but have a strong tendency to revert to the old ways. In town, it will be different. The Two-Law cadre are dedicated to their brainless Two-Law party, and can be expected to attack us on sight."

"With clubs," I offered. "We've got clubs of our own. Tell the troops we're the winning side—just stick together and follow orders and the good old days will be back before long." He did so. They seemed satisfied.

There were civilians standing around a cottage ahead. I sent Lst over to tell them we were the army of liberation. Two young fellows wanted to join up. They had their reservist overcoats, and I let them fall in at the tail of the column. There was a lot of talking in ranks, which was fine with me; they were briefing each other and developing an *esprit de corps*.

More houses, more recruits. There were commercial signs along the road now. Finally we reached a wide area and the village street lay ahead. There were a few people—I realized I had started thinking of the Ylokk as "people"—on the sidewalks. There were a couple of heavy self-propelled carts, loaded with obscure merchandise in bales and boxes. For the first time I got a good look at the Ylokk script, on signs and the sides of carts; it appeared to consist of dotted x's and odd-shaped loops. I hoped I wouldn't have to learn to read it.

Major Lst was beside me, on my left, Andy on my right. "The barracks is at the end of the high street," the captive officer told me. "That's our best bet; there'll be room for all, and it will seem natural enough to the Two-Law die-hards that we should go there with recaptured slaves."

"Could be a trap, Colonel," Helm contributed.

Minnie darted over to the nearest shop window which had a display of bright-colored objects I couldn't identify. She was virtually dancing with excitement.

"Candy," she squeaked, and lapsed into her fluent Swedish, pleading with him to come see the pretty things. He went over, and the two of them went inside. I halted the column.

Andy came back out after half a minute and came over to me. "I need whatever cash these boys are carrying," he told me bluntly. I told the major, and he barked an order, and in a few seconds Andy had an impressive heap of wooden tokens. They seemed to be hand-whittled from a hard, reddish wood, and bore the same x's and loops in the signs.

"Over a hundred zlots," Lst said. "They've been looting, it seems."

Andy returned to the little store and went back inside. I went over to see what was going on. The interior of the small room was brightly lit and full of colorful stuff. Minnie was squealing and picking up one thing after another, hugging it and putting it back. Andy told her to pick what she liked best. She settled on a big, fluffy stuffed animal, what kind I couldn't tell. The shopkeeper, an elderly, gray-muzzled female, was busy pulling out more and more stuff. Andy waved her back and counted out the wooden money. The old dame was chattering but no one was paying much attention. Finally Andy spoke curtly to her and she retired, muttering, while re-counting the take. He told me she'd been asking why a soldier was so interested in little-girl toys. "I told her it was for his little sisters," he said.

We rejoined the troops, Minnie hugging her blue camel or whatever.

"We'll consider the camel our unit mascot," I explained to Smovia and Major Lst, who relayed the information to the rank-and-file, and made a little ceremony of awarding the honor of carrying it to a hardened sergeant (pale blue stripe) who seemed pleased. Lst had them fall in and we proceeded along the street. Nobody paid much attention to us until a short, thick-set rat came out of a door fronting on the street, looked our way, and came strutting over. He had Security written all over him.

"Deal with this fellow," I told Lst. He forged ahead to intercept the Gestapo-type, who impatiently gestured him aside. Instead of yielding, old Lst did his nifty bow-from-the-waist-and-whip-around, knocking the fellow ten feet. He went over and stood over him as he tried to get to his feet from all fours, and barked something at him. The cop crawled away submissively for a few yards, then reared up and ran to the door he'd come out of.

Lst let him go. He came back looking pretty smug. "That was a fortunate encounter," he told me. "He's Lieutenant Drf, on his way to rouse the garrison: reports of groups of escaped slaves roving the area. I told him it was an orientation exercise for the new workers, and we're part of it, and no one is to interfere on pain of strangulation. That should give us a respite."

"Prolly lying," dear old Gus volunteered, bellying up to the Ylokk major. "Prolly told 'em to lay for us at the barracks." Lst stepped back and waved everybody back, leaving just him and Gus, faced-off. I could see it coming, but Gus was still a slow learner, of course. The torso-sweep doubled him over, gagging; then he sat down and started to bluster between heaves. I told him to shut up and fall in.

Lst caught my eye. "You understand, Colonel, that the veracity of a royal officer is not to be impugned by such as this."

I nodded. "He won't do it again," I assured him. "Move 'em out."

A few of the townspeople stopped to stare at us. A sleek young female with a gathering basket ran out and approached Smovia, offering him something from the basket. Apparently it was food; he sniffed it, made gracious "thank-you-kindly" gestures and nipped at it, then took a good bite. It appeared to be a fruit, rather like a dried apricot. Then, still chewing, he hurried over to me.

"Colonel," he blurted, "the young lady is sick—I can smell the rotten-orange odor—and after her kindness . . . This is delicious—try it!" He offered me the food. "Please, sir," he was begging, "allow me to administer my vaccine—it could save her life!"

Minnie had come over to investigate the excitement. "Unca Mobie is good," she told me appealingly. "Uncanul, say 'Ja visst, det går bra.' Please, Uncanul."

"Sure, good idea," I said, and halted the column. Now I was gnawing on the tough chewy fruit—or whatever it was. I gave the rest to Minnie. She snapped it up and made gleeful sounds like any happy ten-year-old. Smovia went back to the lady with the basket, used sign language and a few words of Ylokk to get her to sit down on a handy brick wall. He turned back her mantle to expose her densely-pelted forearm and rummaged in his little black bag of tricks. She watched spellbound, but made no complaint when he took out the hypospray, put it to her wrist, and blasted a dose of vaccine into her flesh. He called Lst over.

"Tell her to go home at once, and lie down," he instructed the puzzled officer. "She's to eat nothing. I'll try to see her tomorrow."

Lst was backing away from her, but he passed on Doc's directions.

"We can't come close to her," Lst told Doc. "She has the Killing. I can smell it. She's dying."

"Maybe not," Smovia told him. "See that she does as I said. Follow her, find out where she lives." He was all packed up and ready to proceed.

21

We made it to the barracks without any further adventures; it was a long, narrow bunkhouse with a strong ratty smell. Lst went in, preceeded by Sergeant Dvd. There were a few local troops in the building; they left by the back door at a run. The major came back out, looking pleased.

"No problem, Colonel," he said. "And I think I can recruit most of these fellows, if you'll excuse me." Without waiting for my approval, he yelled for Dvd and sent him after the dispossessed soldiers. We settled in, after throwing out the ratty-smelling bedding. The bunks were too narrow, but we were tired.

I stood the first watch and was relieved by Helm after an interminable two hours. Nobody bothered us. Then I slept like the dead. I awoke when Sergeant Dvd came back with another non-com in tow and the ousted troops straggling behind, re-

ported that the cadre, twenty-five recruits, trained
as well as the Ylokk knew how to train a soldier (at
least they knew how to come to attention and fall
in and do close-order drill), were all in favor of a
return to the Old Ways. There was a lot of talk as
each one explained to the others how he'd been
forced to cooperate with the Two-Law intruders.
They were curious about us humongs, who they
couldn't really believe weren't dumb animals until
I got fed up and chewed them out in my broken
Ylokk. Then they got busy and briefed our original
contingent, most of whom they knew, on late
developments.

By dusk, we had a good, tight organization,
apparently eager to go. The Two-Law cadre were
holed up in what had been the town's best inn.
They would be our first target.

"Colonel," Helm addressed me, worriedly, "I
thought the Two-Laws were going to attack *us*.
Major Lst said—"

Just then the nearest window exploded inward
and a paper-wrapped brick *thud!*ded on the barracks floor beside us. Helm unwrapped it and
showed the wrapping to the major.

Lst glanced at the close-packed writing and
threw it aside. "The fools! That's a standard 'Re-
ward For Escaped Slaves' notice, with some blood-
curdling threats scribbled at the bottom. I'm
mentioned by name: it seems I'm an enemy of the
Folk, a traitor, a thief, a liar, and so on!" I could
hear his teeth gnashing.

"We'd best prepare, Colonel," he said tautly.
"The scum will assault the barracks."

"Will they wait until dark?" I asked him.

He shook his head. "This kind don't like night
operations," he dismissed them. "I propose, Colo-

nel," he went on, diffidently, "that I organize my troops in defensive posture, and that we await their assault. It would be foolish to sally forth and expose ourselves needlessly."

I agreed with him, and he got busy lining up the crowd of Ylokk troops from the three different units, getting them in ranks and counting off. He set them to work piling up bunks across the middle of the barracks as defensive breastworks. They were too low for humans; I pointed that out and they stacked them a little higher. I was wondering what kind of assault he was expecting from a force without projectile weapons.

"They have a supply of captured firearms," he confided. "These fellows are all veterans of the, ah . . ."

"Slave-raids," I supplied. About then the artillery preparation began, only it consisted of massed small-arms fire instead of fifty-millimeter rifles. We all hit the deck as the side walls exploded inward in a hail of wood-and-glass chips.

That phase only lasted for a few seconds; then Andy stuck his head up, and I yelled at him, but he called, "They're moving up, sir! I can get one—" and fired. Smovia and I joined in, as well as a few of our native levies who had pistols. I had to call them off and remind them to fire only at easy targets to save ammo, of which we had little. This was a strange idea to the Ylokk, who were used to their no-reload energy weapons.

I saw a rat-snout poke up above the ruined end-wall a few feet from me, a bold Two-Law trying to sneak around right-end. Andy and I fired at the same moment, and the head disappeared in a splatter of brains and other debris. Then another appeared and was also blasted instantly. By then, all our guns were firing; apparently the Two-Laws assumed their initial volley had killed everything inside, and were moving in quite casually to mop up.

Instead, we moved out, our pistols picking them off in windrows, while the local boys moved out past us and went to work with their clubs. They grabbed the handguns the enemy had dropped and joined in the turkey shoot. In five minutes, the Two-Laws were gone, either dead, fled, or in the case of two sergeants and a captain, surrendered. All three of them were talking at once, proclaiming their loyalty to the Jade Palace, and claiming they were forced to serve the Two-Law.

"I don't doubt their sincerity," Lst told me, "now that they see the Two-Laws are losers."

We had so many troops now, the situation was getting unwieldly. I told Lst to divide them up into four squads, platoons, companies, or whatever size unit fit best; then I told Gus and Ben to take command of two of them, and Andy and I took the other two. I asked Marie to take care of Minnie. Both of them complained at not being included in the assault force, pointing out that they'd done their part in the fighting so far.

I explained to them that we were going on the offensive now, and that from now on things wouldn't be so easy. Meanwhile, the enemy attack had petered out completely.

My plan was to launch two companies in a direct frontal assault on the warehouse where most of the fire was coming from; meanwhile the other two groups would go out the back, swing wide left and right, and come back and hit the warehouse from both sides at once. Andy pointed out that it wasn't much of a plan, but he admitted he had nothing better to offer.

Smovia was busy giving quick physicals to all our troops, who lined up docilely and submitted to his poking and thumping. He found two in the early stages of the Killing, and quarantined them in one end of the long barracks, after inoculating them.

When I couldn't stall any longer, I had my company fall in, and we went out in a single file, which was all the narrow door allowed; then we did a column-right, halted, and left-faced.

There were a few unaimed shots from the warehouse. We ignored that, and started off double-time, holding our fire until we had targets, visible through the open doors, skulking outside their refuge. The fire picked up a little, but not much. The Two-Law levies seemed to have lost what little enthusiasm they'd had.

We reached the warehouse. We didn't slow down, but ran in through the big wide-open, garage-type doors and slammed into a mass of Ylokk huddled in the center of the big room. They were in a hurry to surrender; our boys had to crack a few heads, and there was a little snapping and biting, but none of them used their firearms.

The arrival of the two flanking parties was anticlimactic; the fighting was all over before they got there. Lst had an earnest talk with pink-striped Captain Blf—the one in charge of the garrisons—and reported back that the entire unit was ready, even eager, to attack the "real" Two-Laws, the group of only about thirty dedicated rebels who had invaded the town in the very beginning.

There were no casualties on our side, except for a few contusions and a couple of bites. Doc got busy and patched them up. Good old Gus had a bruised shoulder; he was skulking and complaining about fraternizing with rats. He got louder and louder, demanding that he be allowed to shoot the rat that had bitten him, whom he claimed he could recognize by the black stripe down his back.

Lst asked Captain Blf about that. "A full colonel? Here? Why?"

Blf went off and picked the colonel out of Smovia's clutches (he had a crease in his scalp Gus had given him in the process of getting himself bruised). Lst then questioned him very respectfully. He seemed puzzled; the colonel answered him readily enough, but seemed to be evasive at times.

"He's being cagey," the major reported. "There's something going on he doesn't want to talk about, but he gives himself away by his seemingly erratic pattern of avoidance. I'm a well-trained interrogator, Colonel; any casual questioner wouldn't have caught it."

"Keep after him," I directed. "Meanwhile, we have a town to liberate—or to inform that they're already liberated."

While Lst and I were making preparation to send out well-armed squads of three to spread the word, and incidentally locate useful supplies, Smovia came over and asked to go along, to identify the sick, and start getting them into some sort of improvised clinics until he could get to them.

"I'll have to train some people to help me," he confided. "I trust I have your approval, Colonel."

I told him to go ahead, but to look sharp for trickery. He assured me he wasn't interested in suicide, and showed me the heavy revolver he'd become attached to. "I'll use it if I have to," he assured me.

*   *   *

It was time for a council of war. I called the humans together, plus the Ylokk officers and noncoms, as I'd be relying heavily on them; not *too* heavily, I hoped. But the troops seemed to be highly motivated, especially since the attack, such as it was, on the barracks had showed them how willing their erstwhile comrades had been to fire on them.

"We have to be careful," I told them, "not to be overconfident: so far we haven't really faced any determined opposition by organized units, such as we can undoubtedly expect in the city."

Major Lst wanted to say something, mainly to us humans: "My people," he began, "though not practiced in the arts of war, are not lacking in intelligence, or in courage. It was Grgsdn who observed the constant strife among the humongs in those phases dominated by them; that gave him, he said, the concept of taking by force that which we desired—and what more desirable than a source of intelligent and vigorous slaves, to perform those chores that are 'beneath the dignity of the Folk,' as he put it. The response was astonishing. First hundreds, then thousands flocked to hear him screaming his message of the eternal holiday; no more work, forever—coupled with an unheard-of abundance of every kind of desirable goods."

"That's an incredibly naïve concept," Smovia commented. "Did he imagine these fierce warriors he so admired could not resist?"

"His intent was to overwhelm with numbers," Lst explained. "Plus the new 'weapons'—we had no word in our language—which rendered our troops irresistible, he declared."

"And," Helm contributed, "he could hardly expect to install his New Order until he had eliminated the old; thus the revolution and the kidnapping of little Minnie."

"He must have remarkable charisma, this Grgsdn," I remarked. "What's he like?"

Lst didn't know; he'd never seen him. Few had, it seemed; none in our army. His disciples spread the word, but Grgsdn himself stayed in hiding, adding the allure of mystery to his appeal.

"They were fools," Lst snarled, "but please believe me: they are not representative of the Folk in general. The great majority would gladly return to the old ways, if there were a way. We shall provide that way."

We talked it over at length and decided to move in openly, in a single column, with the human personnel in the center. Let the Two-Laws wonder what was happening. We'd surround and neutralize any detachment of Two-Law militia we encountered, and enlist as many as possible before moving on. We'd advance directly to the Skein technical compound and secure it, then invest the Palace, and relieve the Loyalists still defending it. When calm had been restored, we'd cap our *fait accompli* with the presentation of Her Highness the Princess.

"Then, maybe," Gus grumbled, "we can give some thought to our *own* problems."

"When we have secured the technical facilities," I pointed out, "we can immediately put an end to the flow of reinforcements for the invasion, *and* arrange for our own return home. And *only* when we hold the compound," I emphasized. Finally old Gus had stopped griping, partly because of the belated realization that there would be no massacre of "rats," and partly because he was beginning to understand that it really wouldn't be a good idea.

Smovia, having administered his medicine to all the sick troops in our bunch, was more relaxed, and indeed eager to get on with it. For their part, the soldiers, seeing their dying comrades restored to full health, tended to regard the Doc as a magician, and to be *very* protective of him. I felt a little bad about what I had to do.

We commandeered backpacks from the supply-room attached to the barracks, packed them with food, sleeping gear, and whatever else anybody wanted to carry. In a shed behind the supply-room, there was a cache of human-made clothing and small items like watches and pocket-knives. Lst told us it was a two-mile hike to the center of town. We started at dawn, well-rested, watered and fed. Three fellows were still sick and we left them behind.

22

The inner-city wall was high and impressive, stoutly built of hewn stone with spikes on top. The gate was of plank-and-iron-strap construction, and guarded by a tall Ylokk in a fancy red-and-gold outfit, and armed with a Bofors hand-cannon he didn't seem to know how to hold. He kept peering down the three-inch barrel while fiddling with the firing mechanism. His head was still intact, however, when I followed Major Lst up to him. He gave the major a casual look, and switched his gaze to me, until Lst barked what sounded like "Hsst!" followed by a rusty-spring squeal. Then the sentry snapped-to and almost dropped the cannon. Lst grabbed it and checked it over expertly.

"Fine weapon," he commented to me. "Clever recoil mechanism."

I agreed and helped him find the ceremonial-looking but functional key attached to the sentry's belt, and we got the gate open. Nobody jumped out and said "Boo!," and we filed through unchallenged. I had the humans out as flankers now. The Jade Palace loomed, pale green as a jade palace should be, replete with crenellated towers, slim spires, flying granfallons, and ominous fire-slit openings through which their devastating disruptors could be aimed.

We came on like people who belonged there, and, following Lst's directions, took the drive that swept around the side to the technical compound out back. A few Ylokk in lab coats who were lounging around outside the big front door looked curiously at us, but nobody made a move.

We bypassed the main entrance and took a footpath around to a small entry almost hidden by pink flowering shrubs. There were two businesslike Ylokk here in combat fatigues. They unlimbered two-foot clubs and hung loose, watching us approach. Then the one with the green back-stripe squealed something and Lst replied with a squeal of his own. He spoke softly and both of the guards snapped-to, turned to unlock the door, and disappeared inside.

"What were the magic words?" I asked him.

"I told them the truth," he said. "They know me, of course. We are the escort of Her Highness. I gave the impression her retinue would be along shortly—" He broke off because the advance guard of a howling mob burst into view coming around the other side of the building. They had clubs and looked plenty mad.

Swft suddenly appeared at the front of our column. As soon as he had realized who we were, he had broken his cover and joined us. Taking in the situation, Swft went to meet the mob. A tall Two-

Law sergeant in the front rank raised his club. Swft took it away from him and barked an order. Some of the oncoming crowd shied away from him and flowed past on both sides.

Smovia whistled softly and said, "That is one *tough* rat."

"Look out, Swft!" I yelled, and moved up, with Helm beside me, to take out a couple of enterprising Two-Laws who had ducked in behind the general. But two more rushed him from the flank; he nailed one with the borrowed club and the other backed off, just in time for another pair to volunteer from his right. Andy and I intercepted them, and old Gus charged past us and took the offensive.

Swft was surrounded by the mob now, and taking solid blows from numberless clubs. Major Lst worked his way through to him and took a position back-to-back with the general. They clobbered Two-Law after Two-Law, until they were surrounded by a ring of fallen attackers.

Gus slammed through to them, and was felled by a big Ylokk with a six-foot quarterstaff. Helm got ahead of me, and I had to call him to heel.

"Don't get cut off, Andy," I cautioned him. By then I was close enough to knock the wind out of a Two-Law who was squarely behind the lieutenant and winding up for a killing blow to the head. There were plenty of targets; we kept busy knocking them over, and in a few seconds were climbing the ring of casualties with Gus, to join Lst and Swft.

The latter gave me a grateful glance and said, "We must break out of this trap before it occurs to them that one blast from a disruptor would finish us all." He glanced toward our troops, who, surrounding the Princess, Marie, and Smovia, had interlocked their short arms and had been backed against the wall near the door.

"Her Highness—" he started, and staggered at a blow delivered by a squatty pink-striper who had noticed his distraction. I slammed the attacker down and another behind him.

Swft was back beside me. "We must relieve Her Highness!" he managed to gasp out. Ylokk lungs didn't have our human capacity for prolonged effort. I nodded, and we formed a retiring wedge and roved our way back to the group guarding the princess in the partial shelter of the doorway. The assault was slacking off; the Ylokk lacked sticktoitiveness.

"Your Highness!" Swft called. "Retire inside, I beg of you! Nst," he addressed the non-com in charge of the detail. "Inside! At once!" Then to me, "The lock will be difficult." Nst went right to work on it with a tool of some sort, but seemed to be having no success. Too bad; the mob was pressing us hard. We needed an escape route.

Intent on all this, both Helm and I failed to intercept a Two-Law who plunged in from the flank and dealt Swft a terrible blow with a three-foot club. Swft didn't fall, but staggered aside, and was surrounded by the enemy, who pulled him down and flowed over him.

Andy shot two or three and charged; I nailed a fellow who slipped in behind him, and we reached Swft, or what was left of him. He looked like a rolled carpet, oozing blood. The poor fellow had never fully recovered from that first shot back at the transfer station before the beating he had taken at the hands of the mob; and now this trampling. I tried to get an arm under him to help him up, but Smovia was right: Swft was one tough rat.

He pulled from my grasp and brushed Andy aside, and reared up to his full seven-foot-two, and yelled at the mob of Two-Laws surrounding us: "Get back! I order you in the name of Her Imperial Highness: withdraw!"

I understood what one fellow right next to me yelled back: "Give us the slaves!"

Swft pushed forward and struck the impudent Two-Law down. The mob shuffled uncertainly. Some seemed ready to attack; others were moving back. They were balanced on a knife edge.

"These humongs are under my protection!" Swft shouted, and knocked down another pushy Two-Law. The next fellow started a lunge toward the general, and I tripped him and then stamped on his head. Swft was still on his feet, but sagging. He delivered a buffet to still another aggressive rat, and was at once assaulted from two sides. Andy and I fired into these, making every shot count.

Old Gus moved up and added to our firepower. We beat them back, though they didn't seem to learn very quickly that our pistols were lethal. A Two-Law sergeant lying at Swft's feet stirred, and before I could nail him, lunged upward with a foot-long knife, trying to rip Swft wide open, but only slashed his thigh. Swft fell, bleeding copiously.

Minnie had slipped past her soldier guard; she came up beside me. The mob fell back then, quieting down as if even they were stunned at the enormity of attacking Her Highness. Andy pulled her back, and Smovia went to Swft, while Big Gus and I took turns clubbing down any of the mob who tried to approach. There was the ear-shattering *bang!* of a pistol shot behind us, and I turned to see Ben ready to fire again into the lock, but Nst kicked the door and it swung in as pieces of the lock mechanism dribbled from its edge.

"Have to get him inside!" Smovia yelled. He was tugging at General Swft's ankles. I gave him a hand.

"Guess that rat's done for," Gus yelled in my ear. "Guess maybe now we can go in there and get at the machine that'll take us back where we belong."

"Help the doc get him inside," I ordered him. He griped, but Ben and Marie stepped in to help. Andy and I, as well as Smovia, had our hands full. We could go on heaping up Two-Laws with headaches, but they kept on coming. We were saving our ammunition for the ultimate emergency.

"What you want with a dead rat?" Gus demanded, then ducked a club swung by a rat who stepped on Swft's inert body. "Whyn't we get inside and get gone?"

"He gave his life for us," I said. "We owe him something."

There seemed to be almost a lull in the assault. Our soldiers were still staying close around Minnie, or trying to. She slipped between two of them and right past me and advanced a step, then another, toward a captain in the glowering, shouting front rank of the mob. She held out a somewhat bedraggled bouquet of the wildflowers she had been gathering along the way. The dumfounded Two-Law officer took the offering and abruptly went to all-fours.

"Her Highness!" he yelled. "It's Her Highness!" He crept backward, then rose and issued commands. The mob began to melt away. He prostrated himself again and waited, crouched before the young rat-girl.

"Rise, loyal soldier," she said to him, as one to the manor born. What was it, I wondered—instinct, developed over millennia of exercising absolute authority?

Minnie raised her voice: "Go to your house now," she called.

Smovia was back, looking distressed. "They'll tear her limb from limb," he bleated.

"Not while I live," a sleek young captain of her self-appointed guard said. He moved up beside her, and quietly urged her to retire. Meanwhile, a cry had gone up: "Her Highness! Her Highness! She's come back! It's Her Highness!"

"Come on, Colonel," Helm urged. "It's time to get inside." The rest were already past the broken-open door, and Andy and I slipped inside the Skein compound accompanied by confused yells from the Two-Law-led crowd.

"Where is Her Highness?"

"—lies! Don't be fooled!"

"I saw her!"

"—a plot to deceive us all!"

"You're insane, you know, Mister Colonel," good old Gus told me, "if you think you're going to make that crowd knuckle under to a baby rat. How do you plan to do it?"

It was dark and cooler inside the technical facility. All I could see was lab-type benches and a corridor leading off into the rear of the building. I didn't give old Gus an answer because I didn't have one. I'd been counting on Swft to handle that part. Now he was flat on his back, or as flat as his anatomy would allow; Smovia was stitching up his eighteen-inch wound.

"How bad is he, doctor?" I asked him. He nodded impatiently, "No real damage done," he muttered. "Lost lots of blood, of course, but septicemia is his big risk. I've used plenty of antibiotics, and he *could* pull through."

"Not in time to help much, Colonel," Andy remarked.

"Damn right!" Gus chimed in. Andy socked him in the gut and he shut up, momentarily. As soon as he recovered his wind he was grabbing at my arm and telling me, "We got to get out of here, now!"

"And what of Her Highness?" Major Lst spoke up. "We've come this far; we can complete the mission."

"*My* mission," Gus cut in, "is to get my sweet butt back to Södra, where it belongs!"

He looked toward poor little Minnie, where she was huddled by the door, surrounded by her faithful guardians. She stood and spoke to a fellow beside her, who almost fell down prostrating himself and unbarring the door. Before I could get my jaw open to yell, she had slipped through into the mob-roar and a glimpse of angry rat-faces. I got to the door with my pistol unlimbered, and watched her step up on the pediment of a fancy lamppost and face the crowd: The noise abated enough for me to hear her say, in that little-girl voice:

". . . return to your homes, as I shall, now."

Smovia jumped forward to dissuade her. She stepped aside from his clutch and said, "It's all right, dear Unca Mobie. I know what to do."

They gave way as she stepped down; there was some scuffling in the front rank between a few diehards who were still out for blood, and the cooler heads, who, being in the majority locally, suppressed the agitators. A lane opened up right across the lawn to the elegant green tower looming over the Skein terminal.

We all watched with our mouths open as she went up the broad steps to the ornate doors; all but her self-appointed escort, who hurried to form up alongside her, while the crowd took up the chant:

"Her Highness is here! Welcome to the Empress!"

Then they set up a discordant wailing that Lst told me was the anthem of the Folk. By now a pair of well-groomed rats in fancy overlong coats with brocade-and-lacework had appeared at the palace doorway, and were ushering Minnie respectfully inside.

Andy muttered a sound expressing admiration and astonishment. "Talk about class!" he commented. "And this Grgsdn thought he could replace *that!*"

Swft had gotten to his feet, his leg tightly bandaged. Smovia was fluttering like a mother bird, but the general pushed him back.

"I must be at the side of Her Highness!" he insisted. "There is much that I can explain—matters which *require* explication!"

"Try explaining some of it to us," Andy suggested.

"That child," Swft stated impressively, "is the legitimate heir the mob has been howling for, spurred on by the traitors of the Two-Law party and by Grgsdn, its infamous leader. Her return will put an end to the rebellion, and"—he caught my eye and paused impressively—"to the foolish invasion attempt."

"OK if we get out of here now?" Gus came in on cue. "I guess the little pet rat—" He got that far before Major Lst gave him the old torso-sweep and slammed him back against a flimsy partition, which collapsed. Gus, cursing loudly, extricated himself from the shattered screen, not without a few cuts from the broken glass.

"Looky here what that rat done to me!" he demanded, holding out a burly forearm bleeding from a number of superficial cuts. "Done cut me up some," he concluded, then resumed yelling. Andy had to sock him hard under the ribs to quiet him down. He finally ran out of gas, and huddled, whimpering amid the debris.

Major Lst and I had succeeded in restraining Swft.

"We'll go over later, sir," the major reassured his superior. "When things have calmed down a bit. But how *did* Her Highness—if she really *is* Her Highness—come to be wandering in the forest in the company of escaped slaves?"

"We're not escaped slaves," I told him. "We're with the Army of Occupation, or the Imperial Embassy, depending on how the details are sorted out."

"Salubriously, I have no doubt, Mr. Ambassador," Swft put in. "At ease, Major. I'll brief you later." He was looking anxiously out through the open door toward the Palace entry. The last of the crowd were trailing away across the plaza, carrying their wounded, with only a few scraps of paper and items of dropped equipment to indicate the recent activity.

"I'm worried, Colonel," Smovia told me. "The poor kid is outnumbered. She can only get so far on her youth and innocence."

"Don't forget her instincts," I reminded him. He nodded. "I suppose her clan has ruled here for at least as long as collies have herded sheep—and every collie pup is born with an urge to round up something."

"Ah, Colonel," Ben said diffidently. "Gus was, of course, out of line, but now the little female *is* back in her palace, surely we can give a thought to our own return home."

Swft spoke up. "I heard your noble speech, Colonel, when I lay near death, when you vowed to carry on my mission. I now absolve you of that responsibility; I am after all, alive, thanks to the good doctor, and I can carry on from this point."

"Not quite," I objected. "I want to see little Minnie enthroned in state, and this Grgsdn in irons."

Major Lst spoke up: "Gentlemen, I respectfully suggest that we form up in a military manner and proceed to the Palace as if expecting to be welcomed. The time for killing is past."

He was right, of course. We marched over in formation. The fancy-dress sentries at the big west facade snapped to, and a moment later the liveried footmen inside were holding the ornate door open for us. Official-looking fellows came over and clustered around Swft. He seemed to be reassuring them that all was in order, and motioned me forward. I went up and was introduced to a baron and a duke, and Swft gave me full credit for saving his life, and those of several victims of the Killing. The courtiers got excited then, and questioned him closely. Then the most elaborately-braided of the bunch hurried away as if to spread the word. By now, a new crowd had formed outside, not shouting threats this time, but clamoring for Her Highness who, they shouted, had come back to overthrow the Killing.

Five minutes later, a party of uniformed Ylokk

came marching into the square in good order,
herding along a score or so of battered-looking
fellows with the yellow badges of the hard-core
Two-Law.

Swft conferred with a couple of other red-stripers,
and came over to tell me all organized resistance
to the restoration of order had ceased, and could
he show us to our quarters now?

He could; I, for one, was so tired I couldn't
think, and the rest were in no better shape. It was
the finest bed I'd ever stretched out on; I got that
far in my assessment before I fell over the edge
into dreamless sleep.

23

I woke lying on a hard army cot, with my mouth dry and my stomach complaining of neglect. We ate, cleaned up, and were escorted into the Presence.

Swft, immaculate in a new overcoat with a vivid reddish-purple stripe, was beside me.

"Her Highness made an appearance before her Folk this morning," he told me. "When she appeared on the balcony, she was unanimously acclaimed as the rightful Empress. So we'd best call her 'Her Majesty' now. Order is being restored, and Doctor Smovia's clinic is treating as many of the ill as can make their way there. Later, we'll send out mobile innoculation teams. The Folk feel that Her Majesty has conquered the Killing. The Two-Law party seems to have become very inconspicuous. As for Grgsdn, he's managed to elude my dragnet, and is still hiding somewhere. If any of the escaped 'slaves' find him, he'll meet the fate he deserves."

"What about the invasion?" I wanted to know. Swft assured me that all operations had ceased, except for the schedule of shuttles bringing the troops back home. Other units were being prepared to repatriate all captives.

Minnie looked radiant. She ran to Smovia and hugged him, before being shooed off by a dignified elderly female.

There ensued several days of euphoric mutual congratulations, punctuated by brilliant social events. Finally, I took Swft aside and told him it was time for me to go.

He agreed, and apologized for the delay, but said it had taken time to round up all the escaped humans roving the countryside, and to prepare enough travelers to carry all four hundred nine of them. I was surprised there were so few, but it seemed humans had proved unexpectedly hard to capture. I just had time to see Minnie for a moment and ask her how she felt about a Ylokk–Imperium alliance; she didn't quite know what that was, but when I explained, she was delighted. She'd led a strange life so far, but it hadn't affected her naturally happy disposition, though she did weep a little when she realized Candy and Unca Mobie would be leaving soon. She gave us all fancy starburst medals that would look fine on our dress whites, I thought.

I was asleep in the luxury suite I'd been ushered to. Just before dawn, there was a knock at the barred door. I went over and asked, "Who's there?"

Swft answered, and I opened up. He and a few

other ranking officers moved aside, then he stepped forward and clapped me on the shoulder, and told me,

"All is well, Colonel. Her Majesty requests and requires your attendance, and that of Lieutenant Helm and Doctor Smovia at breakfast on the south terrace in half an hour."

Minnie kept us waiting—about ten seconds. We were standing by the balustrade of the terrace, looking down at the wildflower garden spread out below, with the city beyond and the hills in the distance. The same topography as back home in the Zero-zero line, but a very different place. Even from this distance we could see the volunteer cleanup crews clearing up the trash deposits left in the streets by years—how many no one was quite sure—of Two-Law domination. The former Two-Law bully-boys were doing most of the really dirty work, spurred on by the ungentle citizens whom they'd terrorized for so long.

"That Grgsdn is still at large," Andy remarked, as if reading my thoughts. "He won't take this quietly. He roused the populace once when all was stable and running smoothly. What's to prevent him from doing the same again—like Napoleon's Hundred Days, after he'd been exiled to Elba?"

"The Army is working over the country very carefully, Andy, as you well know," I reassured him. "Surely they'll pick him up soon."

Minnie arrived at a run, and threw herself at Helm. He returned her embrace happily, and for a while they talked baby-talk and stared at each other. She stepped back and did a twirl. "Is not my clothing pretty, Candy?" she demanded.

Then the anxious-looking captain of the guard detachment arrived and got in front of the excited girl and apologetically asked her to remain with the escort. She said she would, and took his hand and patted it. He yanked it back as if she were red-hot. "Majesty!" he choked. "It is not proper!" Then he shut up and backed out of the Presence.

"Prp is such a ninny," Her Majesty Minnie said. She came over and leaned on the balustrade beside me.

"Now, Uncanul," she began before giggling, "I know you want to take your people home; I don't know how Unca Swft and I will manage without you, but we must face that."

"Minnie," I replied, "what's this 'Unca Swft' stuff? Who is he, really?"

"General Lord Swft is my uncle, the Prince Royal," she told me. "He should really be the emperor now; I'm not qualified. My parents, Emperor Wqk and Queen Tzt were assassinated, you know, at the same time I was k-kidnapped." The tears started. I patted her awkwardly, and Marie came over and embraced her.

"Right," Andy said heartily, "Time to go!" He leaned over Marie's shoulder to say:

"Goodbye, Baby: I know you'll be a marvelous sovereign. I have to go now."

"Candy," she wailed, and Captain Prp was there in an instant, eyeing Helm with hostility, one thin-fingered hand hovering over the butt of his disruptor pistol. Minnie blinked back the tears and said, "Captain, if I ever again discern on your face an expression of less than total respect and affection for our honored guests, it will be permanent latrine detail for you. Begone!"

He stumbled away, and I covered my confusion

by blocking off old Gus, who was pushing forward with his big mouth all ready to start braying about "time to go."

"Fall in there, Gus," I ordered him. The rest of our little band of heroes formed up our usual square formation, even though its original purpose, the protection of Minnie in the center, was now obsolete. We said some good-byes and went along to Skein Operations. Minnie wanted to come with us, at least that far, but Smovia and Helm managed to dissuade her by promising to come back to visit as soon as possible.

24

The equipment in the big, echoic shed wasn't entirely unfamiliar; at least the feel of the place was the same as that of the Net Garages erected on the same spot back home. I was again, for the thousandth time, aware of how strong the affinities were that existed across all the continua, tying together the multitude of alternate realities arising from a single primordial source. Evidently, the pattern was set in the instant of the Big Bang. I went to the nearest traveler, a twin to the one Swft had lost back in Sigtuna. The first batch of enslaved human captives were already on hand, perhaps a hundred people standing in a confused huddle by a big mass-transfer unit. Gus and I went over and I waved away the instant bombardment of questions in a dozen languages.

"We're going home," I told them, while Ben conferred earnestly with some of the slaves with

229

whom he and Marie had worked. They quieted down, and I went on to tell them that the war was over and there was no need to kill the Ylokk technicians working nearby, and that they were, in fact, preparing our transport. A small, ferret-like fellow in a yellow smock came over and introduced himself as Technician-in-Chief Plb, and asked if I would care to inspect the transport. I would. I told Andy to keep our passengers together and quiet, and I went and looked over the big, boxy machine, just like the one I'd seen back in Stockholm Zero-zero, discharging Ylokk troops into the city streets. It wasn't luxurious, but there was room for all on the padded benches, and the front office was manned—or Ylokked—by a competent-looking fellow who reported all systems go. I waited until the rescuees were loaded and then waved our party into the smaller unit I'd picked for our own use.

"What about all the others?" Smovia wanted to know. "I heard you talking to Swft about repatriation, but failed to gather the gist of the matter."

"In return for the lessons you gave to the volunteers," I told him, "Swft agreed personally to see to the orderly return of all captive humans to their respective points of origin. The last traveler will carry a cargo of gold bars as partial compensation to them for their inconvenience."

"Do you think we can really trust Swft, once we're gone?" Helm wondered.

"I'm certain of it," I answered him, "and so is Minnie." I looked at Smovia and the others.

"Sure," they agreed. "Her Majesty will see to it."

"But what about this Grgsdn?" Andy demurred. "He could still start trouble."

I wasn't paying much attention; I was looking at something over in a roped-off corner of the big shed. I strolled over for a closer look. Tarps were hung from some ropes to afford a half-hearted gesture toward privacy. I went between the tarps and was looking at an old-fashioned (maybe twenty years out-of-date) model Net Shuttle. It was partly disassembled, apparently under study by the Ylokk. It was thickly covered with dust, so it had been here the best part of that twenty years.

"Wonder what *that* is," Gus muttered beside me. I had noticed him trailing along and said nothing. He went past me and peered into the warped interior.

"No room in there for a man to breathe, hardly," he commented.

I went over beside him. "Time to tell all," I informed him. "Start with how you deserted from a probe mission after it had blundered into Zone Yellow, and how the closest the Ylokk could come to pronouncing 'Gunderson' was 'Grgsdn.' "

"Crazy as hell," old Gus remarked. "You seen yourself, I was a slave here, just like all the other folks. Ask Ben and Marie. They'll tell you."

"We wondered about Gus," Marie spoke up. "Come up to us the day after we slipped off into the woods, all important and bossy, he was. Had a rat with him, but he sent it away. Acted like he was capturing us. In good with the rats, too. Acted like he hated 'em, but we could tell he'd thrown in with them. Damn traitor!"

For gentle Marie, that was quite a speech. Ben was nodding his head, but didn't say anything. Old Gus took a swing at Marie that missed because I left-hooked him in the gut.

"Got no call—" he gasped. "I done nothin'. 'Cept brain as many rats as anybody else!"

"You found a peaceful gathering society here," I told him. "You started trouble by telling them they were fools to work when they could have all the work done for them. You hatched the idea of a mass invasion of your home locus, to scoop up as many slaves as possible in a hurry, and settle back and watch them do all the work."

"Plain sense," Gus grunted. "Plenty of idle folks back home never had no use for me; jest set around and enjoyed life while the likes o' me broke my back doing all the hard labor. Same thing here. This damn 'Jade Palace' stuff, and the big shots living high—and then I seen a chance. Rumors started about no heir to the throne: I never started 'em, but I give 'em all the help I could. Lotsa folks listened when I first started making speeches. I was a curiosity, you see, they never seen a critter like me before. Thought I knew it all. Revered me, like. There's always folks'll listen to somebody telling 'em they got a bad deal. Then I went underground and left it to my followers. And I got even with alla the fancy folks treated me like dirt!"

"Overthrowing a government in Zone Yellow is hardly a punishment for the educated classes back in the Zero-zero line," I told him. "Most of them have never heard of Zone Yellow."

Gus grunted. "Damn blood-suckers!"

"The Ylokk were quick studies," I reminded Gus. "They duplicated the shuttle circuitry and began their own exploration of what they decided to call the Skein."

"Not *my* fault," Gus muttered.

"You saw your chance for what seemed to be

the perfect revenge on society," I went on, ignoring his head-shaking and dismissing motions. "You'd lead the Ylokk back home, and they'd loot and enslave the very people who had rejected you."

He came closer, a sorrowful look on his blunt features. "Naw, feller, you got that wrong. I never—" He interrupted himself to try a sneaky right jab, which I blocked with my left; then I hit him on the point of the chin hard enough to put a glaze on his eyes. He dropped like a sack of meal. Funny thing about old Gus, he always complained when I socked him, but he never hit back. This time he was out cold.

The others had gathered around to ask questions. I gave them a brief explanation, and Ben and Marie nodded knowingly. "Explains a lot of things about Gus," she said. "He knew all about the invasion, and a lot of other stuff. Asked him how he knew so much about what the rats were planning, and he just laughed."

"We thought maybe he was a spy for the rats at first," Ben added. "He walked in on us when we were hiding out, and just sort of took over, noisy. Wasn't much scared of the rats finding us. Said he had their number. We finally got him quieted down, and once we got into the woods he didn't have much to say. Marie and I were thinking about ditching him when we ran into you folks."

"Colonel," Andy said, in an uncertain tone, "how much time has passed? How long have we been away? Doc and I were in that hut for a good ten years, but you said—"

"To me, it seemed like perhaps a couple of weeks," I told him. "I don't know. When we begin meddling with the time/space/vug equations, strange things can happen. In normal Net travel, if I can use the word for something as out-of-the-ordinary as the M-C drive, temporal parity is carefully retained. The circuits are balanced specifically for that purpose. But we've ducked in and out of temporal stasis, changed machines—we don't know how temporally stable the Ylokk transports are—so we've probably built up at least a slight discrepancy. Not too great, I hope."

"There's no telling what's been happening back home," Andy remarked. "Who do you think is winning, Colonel?"

"I'm sure we are," I told him. "Especially since we cut off the supply of reinforcements."

We trussed old Gus up like a Christmas turkey and got back to the business at hand.

"Do we take him along, Colonel?" Andy asked. I told him Gus would get a fair trial if the Palace faction found him here. We stowed him out of the way in the cargo bin.

"You'll be comfy here for a few hours, Gussie," Helm told him. "Until the Palace guards find you."

He couldn't answer with the gag we'd tied in his mouth, but he rolled his eyes a lot.

I made a final check of the alien instrument readings, not all of which I understood, and threw in the big main drive lever.

I had warned everybody they'd feel a strange sensation as the field took hold, but they'd all felt it before and lived through it, and in a moment it passed.

All these machines had been designed for the sole purpose of travel between Zone Yellow and the Zero-zero line, so there was no navigation to worry about. We watched the red line on the big chronometer as the needle moved closer, and when they coincided, the drive cut automatically.

"Home!" Helm said reverently. I tried various controls, trying to activate the external-view screens, but got nothing. The only thing left to do was open up.

Helm did that, and I said "Hold it!" before he stepped out. The next instant a shot *whang!*ed off the outer hatch, followed by a fusillade. Helm stepped back, looking bewildered.

"My mistake, Lieutenant," I said. "By now NSS has surrounded the warehouse the Ylokk were using as a reception depot, and are in position to attack any arriving Ylokk transport before it can discharge its troops. They don't know who we are, of course."

We rigged up a flag of truce and stuck it out. It was shot to pieces at once.

Then the firing stopped and I called: "Lay off! We're friends!"

"Brion?" a voice called back. "Brion! Is it possible?" I recognized Manfred's voice, but he sounded weak and uncertain. I stepped out into the big, empty warehouse. Armed NSS men stepped out of concealment, keeping me cornered. An old man rushed forward, and just before he embraced me I recognized him as Manfred.

"How long?" I managed to get out as he talked excitedly.

"—when you didn't return after the agreed two weeks—"

"I don't remember that," I cut in. "But how long *has* it been? Barbro—"

"Brion, after . . ."

"Yes? After . . . what? How long?" I couldn't seem to get through to him. He had aged; he was an old, old man, with bleary eyes and a few wisps of white hair. But after all, he'd been in his eighties when I saw him last. Clearly, he was having a hard time assimilating what was happening.

" 'How long?' you ask, Brion," he said at last, when he'd apparently accepted the reality of our presence. "It was eleven years, this month," he told me, "since I sent you off to a terrible fate in Zone Yellow."

"I have a lot to tell you, sir," I said, "but first I want to see Barb. Where is she? Here in the city, I hope."

"Of course you do," he said, more calmly, giving my shoulder one final pat, as if to reassure himself I wasn't an illusion. "Brion," he said brokenly, "I must tell you; as well to do so at once. The lovely Barbro is not here.

"I apologize, Brion," he went on, "for the rude reception. But you must understand—"

"Pretty dumb, barging in here unannounced," I confessed. "How's the war going?"

"The last, isolated pockets are surrendering as fast as we can get to them," he said. "They seem disinclined to pursue the invasion."

"It wasn't really an invasion, sir," I told him, "in the sense of seizing and holding territory. It was a slave raid."

Richtofen gave me a strange look. "Then they're not executing their captives . . . ?"

"No, just putting them to work. What's this about Barb not being here?"

"*Tak Gud*," the old man sighed. I was surprised he'd be so emotional about it.

"I have nearly a hundred of the captives with me," I said, hoping to relieve his distress, but he only gave me a wild look.

"I don't suppose . . . ?" he started, leaving me to wonder what he didn't suppose.

"I'd like to go home, General," I said a trifle impatiently. "I need a hot bath, and—"

"Brion," he cut me off, "I have not been entirely candid with you. Barbro is not at home. She was captured, only a few days after your departure, while leading a raiding party to attack the Ylokk HQ. We had assumed she was dead. Brion, I'm so sorry."

"You've made no effort to rescue her?" I demanded, sounding sharper than I meant to. He shook his head sadly. "After your supposed failure, Brion . . ." he said, and let it go at that. "But—" he resumed, brightening, "since you did not, in fact fail, we can—"

"General," I cut in, impatient with all this conversation, "please prepare a two-man scout with armament B. I'm going alone. I know what to do." Saying that reminded me of the little Empress, advancing so confidently to meet her fate. Manfred was protesting, and at the same time assuring me that a fine new shuttle would be at my disposal in an hour.

EPILOGUE

The trip in was routine, until I noticed a sudden dip in the continuum-integrity sensor, and looked out to see a familiar landscape: the dreary hills, the one road, and the cozy cottage, where I'd met Swft for the second time. I considered the matter in depth for a full microsecond, and phased-in.

I could see the marks in the muddy road where the traveler had settled in last time. How long ago was that, local? I wondered. There were footprints, too—the party that had shot Swft and hurried away—only now the trail led toward the high-tech "cottage." The boys were still here, it appeared; there were no tracks leading away from the little house. I had a passing impulse to go over and check on what was afoot, but I had an urgent job to do, so I resumed my trip to Zone Yellow. There were still plenty of loose ends to tie up before I could report the situation stabilized.

I resisted the temptation to use the view-screen to monitor my progress across the Zone to its centroid at Ylokk. My instruments would tell me when I arrived, unobtrusively, in the alley behind the Skein shops. I'd paced off the distance, as nearly as I could remember, back in the Net Garage.

I checked. I was getting close: city streets. I didn't really have any plan. I intended to play it by ear.

A few more minutes, and my sensors picked up something moving in the Net, close to me, pacing me. I slowed, and it slowed; when I went back to cruise it stayed with me. I tried some evasive action, phasing-in with a line picked at random; I saw it was very close to the nuclear A-line of the Ylokk, so I moved in carefully. Sure enough, his trace disappeared; he'd overshot me. That was a relief.

I nudged the shuttle across the last few feet and dropped it into identity. I needed some fresh air; no extended EVA this time, just a quick look, and off again. After overriding the safety interlocks, I cycled the hatch and looked out at a busy market-place, where people haggled at open-air stalls. There were no rat-corpses and the stink was gone, replaced by a somewhat subtler stink of plain rat. There were no broken windows in sight, no roving bands of looters in the background.

"This means Minnie has consolidated her position and eliminated the Two-Law nuisance," I told myself, glad to hear the news.

Apparently, in this line the warehouse had burned down; I had arrived out in the open. I noticed a fellow with a gray stripe down the back of his overcoat, and I stepped down on the wet cobbles and went over to him.

"Good day, Major," I said in my best Ylokk. He jumped and gave me a searching look, then looked around rather wildly, I thought.

"Who *are* you?" he demanded. "Whoever you are, you shouldn't be here. If the local constabulary notice you—"

"They won't, Major," I reassured him, "unless you give me away. They're busy shopping, and I'm just a strange-looking fellow talking to an officer."

"Yes, of course, but—" He lowered his voice. "I am Major Hsp. Perhaps you're not aware of the situation, sir," he suggested. I agreed I wasn't.

"The remnant of the Two-Law rebels have gone to earth here in this remote phase," he explained. "They blame you humongs, excuse me, humans, for all their troubles, and—"

"Damn right," I agreed. "Why didn't Her Majesty's troops hunt 'em all down?"

"There wasn't time," the major mourned. "We were rounding them up as quickly as we could, and this one crowd—a fanatical group known as the 'Liberation Front,' whatever that means—"

"Just silly malcontents' jargon," I told him. "How did they get past you?"

"They were well organized. Apparently they had spies in the palace and knew every move we made. A party of them got into the technical compound by night, and stole three transports; they shifted off-phase and established themselves in the park, where the rest of them waited. My fellows arrived just as the last of them were dropping out of identity. We traced them here easily enough. This line is very close to the Nuclear one; they'd prepared a refuge. They've gone underground, mingled with the local population, it seems. All we can do for the moment is keep matters under surveillance. However, we have found their transports and immobilized them. They're trapped. The sudden appearance here of a human could destabilize the situation."

"Someone was shadowing me," I said. "Your boys or theirs?"

"Not mine," he told me, "which means they already know you're here. You'd better depart at once—" He cut off as a yell went up across the square. Someone was hoisting a banner that the major explained read KILL THE HUMONGS. He gripped my arm. "Where's your machine?" he squeaked in my ear, over the rising crowd-noise.

I pointed out its position to him, an invisible presence among a group of big packing-cases and lift-vans. He hurried me in that direction. That was all right with me. It was Barbro I was after, not another entanglement in local politics.

"—well clear of the Zone," he was saying. "I can rendezvous with you and discuss—"

"Never mind," I told him. "Now that I know their location, I can call in a strike force to round them up. All I need to do now is get out of here."

Oddly, the folks nearby paid no attention to me; instead they were craning their necks to see what the excitement was about across the market.

Inside again, I asked Major Hsp how things had gone with Her Majesty after her dramatic return.

"She was acclaimed by all," he told me worriedly, "but the story began to circulate she had sold the folk out to foreigners—aliens—in a word, to 'humongs.' They said she had taken a slave as her closest advisor."

"After all, she was raised by humans," I reminded him.

"I wonder who that slave/advisor would be?" he commented. "We rounded up every human slave we could find, and all were sent back to their home lines."

"How did the slave get in solid so quickly?" I asked.

"No one knows," he admitted. "All rumor and innuendo. But, with this untroubled phase from which to operate, the rebel scum can launch a coordinated attack. Until they're extirpated, the Noble Folk will not know peace or security."

He was looking at me expectantly, I thought. So I asked him, "What's that got to do with me?"

"Surely," he replied, "you will wish to assist in this worthy enterprise."

"I have a project of my own," I told him. "Good luck, but I have to go." He made a motion with his hand, and a dozen Ylokk in uniform materialized from the apparently heedless crowd of shoppers, to surround me.

"I require your assistance," Hsp told me. "I regret the necessity to employ force, but if you insist, I shall do so."

"You mean these?" I inquired, as if incredulously, looking at his six bodyguards. "What do you expect half a dozen recruits to do?" I took a step sideways and a quick leg-sweep knocked the nearest enforcer back into a cart loaded with tubers. The two adjacent hard boys closed the gap, putting them close enough for me to grab both of them by one arm and crack their narrow heads together; then I threw them at another, closing in fast. That left two, plus the major. He called off his remaining pair and said,

"Never mind; I see you're not prepared to be reasonable. You may go."

"You're got your signals mixed, Major," I told him. "I just want to make it clear that my cooperation will be voluntary. What do you have in mind?"

"They have a headquarters," he told me, "somewhere in an outlying Phase. I've not yet managed to locate it. I suspect it's a former technical installation of the Governance, taken over and operated by the traitors."

"And . . . ?" I prompted.

"Using your small transporter," he suggested, "it might be possible to locate the HQ undetected. Then, a swift attack, and they'd be marooned, outnumbered, ready to be hunted down at leisure."

"Come on," I said. "I've got an idea." He told his remaining two hard boys to alert somebody named Colonel Lord Twst, and stepped to my side. I escorted him to my sophisticated two-man scout, and ushered him inside.

"There's an isolated transfer station I learned about from General Swft," I told him. "I happened to notice, on the way here, that it's still in use. That could be the Two-Law HQ." He seemed interested all right, eager to go. I checked my back-trail recording and found the locus. It was a five-minute crossing, and we came to rest just as a party of about ten Ylokk in civvies were approaching the lone building.

"Commissioner Wsk," the major identified one of the party. "That's him in the lead—the treacherous moopah! And the others are junior officers of the Guard! The rot was better entrenched than I suspected!"

"Swft could have told you a lot about that," I told him. "Too bad he didn't have a chance to brief you."

"A pity," Major Hsp agreed. "However, their

secret is out, now. It remains only to return to the Palace and denounce the rascals."

"And leave this bunch here, to do as they please?" I queried.

He nodded curtly. "There's no need to bait them here in their stronghold. Let us go, Colonel, without delay."

I almost argued with him, but didn't. The coil was still hot, so we were off in a moment. This time I steered right to the Ylokk Nuclear Line, which put us in the Skein depot, dark, empty, and echoic in the late evening. We used the "VIPs only" tunnel to the Palace next door, and emerged in the basement guardroom. Hsp used the beeper-recall system to assemble a dozen soldiers, well armed with clubs. He gave them—and me—a fast briefing, then he headed for the staff apartment wing.

Old Prince Vmp was indignant when we routed him out of his big, feathery bed, but he seemed oddly fatalistic. "So it's you, Hsp," he grumbled. "I *told* General Ngd you were unreliable. Should have purged you long ago."

Hsp told him to shut up and had the troops truss Vmp up and secure him, head-down, by a rope tied to his ankles, in his garage-sized closet. We left him there trying to curse around the gag in his mouth.

When I commented that security seemed remarkably lax in the Palace, Hsp told me he was in command of the Guard, and had told all hands to be alert for a sneak approach from outside and to ignore any unusual activity inside the Palace itself. Thus, nobody bothered us as we neutralized a couple more of what Hsp assured me were the prime movers in the plot.

We were doing fine until we opened the big, armored door leading to the Royal Apartments. A small force was waiting for us there. I was the first one through the big double doors, and the heavy drapes beyond, and I was looking at old Gus, flanked by a dozen or so uniformed troops.

Gus took time to give me an astonished look and launch into a speech. "*You*, you damned fool! You should have stayed back in Stockholm with all your fat friends! Don't you understand, this is *my* turf?"

I waited patiently for him to pause for a breath, and socked him good and hard in that soft gut. As soon as he collapsed, his loyal bodyguards split, in all directions. Hsp was body-blocking them off from the wide corridor leading to the Royal living quarters. We locked our three captives in a utility closet just outside the big doors and posted two fellows to watch.

I got Gus on his feet and breathing again, and asked him what he was doing there. "I'd heard Minnie was rumored to have a new, human advisor," I told him when he seemed reluctant to discuss the matter.

"Oh, that's right, Colonel," he confirmed eagerly. "Her Majesty won't make a move without my say-so. I—"

"You're a liar," I reminded him. "Minnie knows what a treacherous skunk you are—even if she doesn't know you were behind the revolt in the first place. She wouldn't trust you to supervise the garbage disposal. Speaking of which, I'm considering what to do with you."

"Oh, just let me go now, and I'll overlook this incident," he gushed. "After all, you didn't know—"

I cut that off with another jab to his short ribs.

Hsp told me Her Majesty's personal suite was just down the corridor, and we went there, prodding old Gus along with us.

"She'll kill me," he was telling me, as if that were a consideration that would stop me in my tracks.

"Nonsense," I told him. "If Minnie has a flaw as a sovereign, it's that she's too kind-hearted."

"Not *her*!" Gus gulped. "It's that big red-headed she-devil!"

"The Ylokk don't have red hair," I corrected.

He brushed that off. "I'm not talking about a rat," he corrected me. "You said yourself she had a new human advisor! This damn female showed up here at the palace just a few days ago, just when I was ready to cinch my position. In another hour I'd have been in control of all palace functions, nothing in or out without my order—but then this dame comes along. Seems she'd been demanding to see Her Majesty—and had 'inflicted grievous bodily injury' on anyone that laid a hand on her, so . . ."

By then we were at the sanctum sanctorum, and before Hsp could use his master-key in the door, it opened, and someone tall and red-haired stepped out and into my arms.

Paksenarrion, a simple sheepfarmer's daughter, yearns for a life of adventure and glory, such as the heroes in songs and story. At age seventeen she runs away from home to join a mercenary company, and begins her epic life . . .

ELIZABETH MOON

THE DEED OF PAKSENARRION

"This is the first work of high heroic fantasy I've seen, that has taken the work of Tolkien, assimilated it totally and deeply and absolutely, and produced something altogether new and yet incontestably based on the master. . . . This is the real thing. Worldbuilding in the grand tradition, background thought out to the last detail, by someone who knows absolutely whereof she speaks. . . . Her military knowledge is impressive, her picture of life in a mercenary company most convincing."—**Judith Tarr**

About the author: Elizabeth Moon joined the U.S. Marine Corps in 1968 and completed both Officers Candidate School and Basic School, reaching the rank of 1st Lieutenant during active duty. Her background in military training and discipline imbue The Deed of Paksenarrion with a gritty realism that is all too rare in most current fantasy.

Ranks of Bronze
Alien traders were looking to buy primitive soldier-slaves—they needed troops who could win battles without high-tech weaponry. But when they bought Roman legionaries, they bought *trouble* . . .

Vettius and His Friends
A Roman Centurion and his merchant friend fight and connive to stave off the fall of Rome.

Lacey and His Friends
Jed Lacey is a 21st-century cop who plays by the rules. His rules.

Men Hunting Things
Things Hunting Men
Volumes One and Two of the *Starhunters* series. Exactly what the titles indicate, selected and with in-depth introductions by the creator of Hammer's Slammers.

To receive books by one of BAEN BOOKS most popular authors send in the order form below.

Rolling Hot, 69837-0 ✪ $3.95 . . . . ☐

Hammer's Slammers, 69867-2 ✪ $3.95 . . . . ☐

At Any Price, 55978-8 ✪ $3.50 . . . . ☐

Counting the Cost, 65355-5 ✪ $3.50 . . . . ☐

Ranks of Bronze, 65568-X ✪ $3.50 . . . . ☐

Vettius and His Friends, 69802-8 ✪ $3.95 . . . . . . ☐

Lacey and His Friends, 65593-0 ✪ $3.50 . . . . ☐

Men Hunting Things, 65399-7 ✪ $2.95 . . . . ☐

Things Hunting Men, 65412-8 ✪ $3.50 . . . . ☐

Please send me the books checked above. I have enclosed a check or money order for the combined cover price made out to: BAEN BOOKS, 260 Fifth Avenue, New York N.Y. 10001.

AN OFFER HE COULDN'T REFUSE

They were functional fangs, not just decorative, set in a protruding jaw, with long lips and a wide mouth; yet the total effect was lupine rather than simian. Hair a dark matted mess. And yes, fully eight feet tall, a rangy, tense-muscled body.

She clawed her wild hair away from her face and stared at him with renewed fierceness. Her eyes were a strange light hazel, adding to the wolfish effect. "What are you *really* doing here?"

"I came for you. I'd heard of you. I'm . . . recruiting. Or I was. Things went wrong and now I'm escaping. But if you came with me, you could join the Dendarii Mercenaries. A top outfit—always looking for a few good men, or whatever. I have this master-sergeant who . . . who *needs* a recruit like you." Sgt. Dyeb was infamous for his sour attitude about women soldiers, insisting that they were too soft . . .

"Very funny," she said coldly. "But I'm not even human. Or hadn't you heard?"

"Human is as human does." He forced himself to reach out and touch her damp cheek. "Animals don't weep."

She jerked, as from an electric shock. "Animals don't lie. Humans do. All the time."

"Not *all* the time."

"Prove it." She tilted her head as she sat cross-legged. "Take off your clothes."

". . . what?"

"Take off your clothes and lie down with me as *humans* do. Men and women." Her hand reached out to touch his throat.

The pressing claws made little wells in his flesh. "Blrp?" choked Miles. His eyes felt wide as saucers. A little more pressure, and those wells would spring forth red fountains. *I am about to die. . . .*

I can't believe this. Trapped on Jackson's Whole with a sex-starved teenage werewolf. There was nothing about this in any of my Imperial Academy training manuals. . . .

BORDERS OF INFINITY by LOIS McMASTER BUJOLD
69841-9 • $3.95